ABOUT THE AUTHOR

The author lives with her husband in West London. They have been travelling through time together for quite a while now, gathering experiences of life and learning about the world around them.

Kensington and Chelsea Libraries

3 0116 02133725 6

DAVID
WAS
DIFFERENT

Sally Bundock

The Book Guild Ltd

First published in Great Britain in 2022 by
The Book Guild Ltd
Unit E2, Airfield Business Park
Harrison Road
Market Harborough
Leicestershire, LE16 7UL
Freephone: 0800 999 2982
www.bookguild.co.uk
Email: info@bookguild.co.uk
Twitter: @bookguild

Copyright © 2022 Sally Bundock

The right of Sally Bundock to be identified as the author of this
work has been asserted by them in accordance with the
Copyright, Design and Patents Act 1988.

All rights reserved. No part of this publication may be
reproduced, transmitted, or stored in a retrieval system, in any form or by any means,
without permission in writing from the publisher, nor be otherwise circulated in
any form of binding or cover other than that in which it is published and without
a similar condition being imposed on the subsequent purchaser.

Typeset in 11pt Adobe Garamond Pro

Printed on FSC accredited paper
Printed and bound in Great Britain by 4edge Limited

ISBN 978 1914471 247

British Library Cataloguing in Publication Data.
A catalogue record for this book is available from the British Library.

This book is dedicated to their daughter and her family. They understand that their granddaughters and indeed all children everywhere are of immense value because they are the future, a future where hopefully all are valued regardless of any 'differences' and where mankind values, supports and protects our beautiful planet and all its inhabitants.

ONE

David knew he was different. He was not quite twelve years old and understood that everyone was different in their own special way. He remembered one of his grandads telling him that when he was much younger. However, David knew he was quite a bit different. The year was 2021 and by the end of the summer holidays, he was to realise he was even more different than he had thought back in July when school had broken up. Some days he minded being the odd one out and others he simply did not. Some days he thought being quite a bit different was really rather special.

David's dad was called Robert and he was black. His mum, whose name was Viv, on the other hand, was white and had long blonde hair. David often marvelled how he was simply somewhere in between. This situation was, he knew, not that much different from others. He had some friends who had white mums and dads, and others who had black or brown mums and dads, and some were simply like him. Nobody minded except for a few unpleasant people who said stupid things, but David always stood up for himself and gave a smart reply back. His dad had showed him how to do that. David was happy with his family the way it was; he felt quite special. He had two sets of grandparents, quite a bit different from each other, really. Sometimes he thought he preferred one set and then the other. He sort of wondered, though, whether that depended on what they bought him for his birthday – the indoor basketball hoop or the electronics starter kit. Which did he like best? All very silly, really.

The reason, though, why David really felt different was because somehow or other about two years ago he had started to feel ill. He felt really very tired and started to drink a lot of water. His mum and dad were quite worried about him as previously he had been so full of energy. Anyway, what had happened was that his mum had taken him to see the doctor, and after a couple of visits and tests, which were not at all like the tests at school, he was told he had something called diabetes. David did not really know what that was, but the doctor and his dad explained it to him and gradually he came to understand. Basically, he was not quite like most other kids his age and also, he had to have injections every day. This he didn't mind too much, but what really annoyed him was that his mum or someone else had to do it for him. He really wanted to be able to do them for himself, but somehow or other he couldn't seem to manage it – well, not yet anyway. He had decided that one of his main aims in life was to learn how to do his injections and be comfortable with it.

David was always looking into the future. His dad had once told him about a book and a film called *1984*. It had been written, he was told, about the time his own father was born. The story was all very futuristic. Well, when 2021 was chimed in at midnight – yes, he was allowed to stay up to welcome in the New Year – he thought, *Forget 1984. How futuristic does 2021 sound?*

2020 had not been a good year. It was the coronavirus year. That nasty virus that was such a terrible problem right the way across the world. It was mentioned so much in the news that even quite young children knew how to spell 'Covid-19' when other much easier words to spell escaped them. It had all started at the beginning of the year at a place in China and David remembered how it had gradually crept across the globe, causing dreadful, dreadful trouble. David knew that many people had died, but fortunately, he felt, he had not known any of them and he did not see any of them and so to some extent the most frightening part of the pandemic, as it was called, did not get too close to him. It had, of course, affected his own life quite a lot in a number of ways. His dad, who worked as an accountant, had to work from home for many weeks whilst his mum, who worked part-time in the office in a large department store, was not able to work at all and eventually was made redundant. David's mum and dad then decided that she could afford to stay at home for a while, and in any case, she was keen to get involved in some voluntary work with the local hospice.

Both sets of David's grandparents lived not far away, although in different directions. All four of them were retired and so they stayed home for a lot of the time. His grandfather on his dad's side of the family was really in quite poor health and so life was particularly difficult for him. He spent a lot of time reading, doing crosswords and just watching television. David's mum had helped out by ordering shopping online for both families and so they did not have to go out to shop for food. They limited their outdoor activities to short walks, wearing masks, and spending much time in their respective gardens. David's other grandad was particularly good at growing vegetables and fruit, which came in very handy for everyone. David did not see much of his grandparents during the lockdown weeks. They liked to talk on the phone and do FaceTime, and sometimes David and his parents drove so they could stand outside their houses, a good way from their front doors, to say hello and ask how they were. This worked as good as anything for them. Zoom was suggested, but it never quite worked for them.

No, David did not remember 2020 fondly at all. Because of his diabetes he had had to stay at home for what seemed like forever. He could not go out to play in the park or the woods out by the back of his home and he could not go to school or meet with his friends. The days stretched on endlessly. He did some home-schooling with his mum sitting with him some of the time and he became quite good at Zooming and WhatsApping with his school friends. He knew that lots of, well, really clever people, were trying to find something called a vaccine but that it was a difficult task. Each day on the television there was more news about what was happening, but David did not really want to watch it and would go to his room when the news was on to play on his PC, WhatsApp his friends or even read a book. David was quite fond of reading, really. He found he could easily lose himself in a story and often imagined he was one of the central characters in a plot.

Amidst all the upheaval caused by the coronavirus there was one other major issue that remained in David's mind throughout the year. The death of a man called George Floyd arrested by police in America sparked demonstrations across the globe. David clearly remembered the discussions at home and amongst his friends, both black and white, about all the issues involved. Feelings ran high and many people seemed to forget the danger from the virus and met in large groups, putting their own and others' lives at risk.

The wait for the virus vaccine was long, but after much trial and error the day came when the news had some really 'good news' for a change. The battle against the pandemic had been partly won at a cost, but vaccines had been developed. They been tested and favourable results found. Those most at risk were to be offered the vaccine first. Now well into 2021 life was settling gradually back to what the grownups called the 'new normal', which was the same in a lot of ways but different in quite a few others. No, 2020 had not been a good year, but David, always trying to look on the bright side of things, had high hopes for 2021 – the year he would be twelve!

Once things had settled down again, many months after the pandemic started, David was so pleased to be able to get out and about again, sometimes with friends and sometimes he even liked to go out on his own. He had always been a boy who to some extent enjoyed his own company. He liked to think. To try and puzzle things out. Things he saw around him. 'What does this mean? What does that mean?' The world was an exciting place to him, and in some ways, he longed to be older than he was so that he could have more freedom. Although he always listened to his mum when she said, 'David, you must appreciate and learn from every day's experiences. Be patient. You will be grown up soon enough!'

David's best friend was actually also his cousin on his dad's side. Malcolm, known to everyone as Mal, was also in the same year at school as David, although in a different class. Mal even lived close to David. He lived just ten doors down and so they really saw lots of each other. Mal's dad, John, was a policeman. Mal was the taller of the two, but David was always fond of saying, 'You wait, Mal, I will catch you up because actually my dad is taller than yours!' Then they would both laugh. Mal was simply excellent at football and was in the school team, and to some extent David envied this as even before the diabetes he was not much good at football, but, well, he was better than Mal at other things, or so he thought.

David's other main friends were in his class. Harish, Ali and John were all great fun and lived really close. David also had what he called an interesting neighbour. Her name was Aylea. Yes, she was a girl but, in some ways, not so very different from David. Aylea was also eleven but went to a different school to David. She was a very fast runner and could climb a tree as well as the boys could. She was incredibly clever on her mobile, but Aylea was different too. She had asthma and so had to carry around something called an inhaler with her. So, like David, she was different, but also fun to talk to and interested in everything going on around her.

David did not have any brothers or sisters, but there was one other member of David's family and that was Luna. Luna was the family dog, a German shepherd who had been with the family for seven years since she was a puppy. Luna was loved by all. She was a great friend, especially to David, and he often took her out for a walk on his own. His parents knew that he was safe as Luna had been well trained and would ensure that David was safe if any danger threatened him.

One other important thing in David's life, other than his mobile phone, was his bike. He loved to ride and often went out with Mal to the park and even to parts of the woods. They often took Luna with them and even sometimes Aylea. Quite often, they took food and drink with them and set up temporary camps when they climbed trees. Once they even built a den out of some fallen branches. David did have to be careful, though, because of his diabetes, but Mal understood and together things worked out pretty well.

In some ways David longed for life to be more exciting and he loved to daydream, and he often had very vivid dreams when he slept. He put this down to his injections, although his mum said, 'Not really, David. You just have a busy mind!' Then they would both laugh.

TWO

The summer holidays were almost halfway through. The family had enjoyed a staycation in the West Country just after school broke up. David loved the Cornwall cliffs and beaches. The boat trip out to the Scilly Isles was magical if the sea a little too rough for his mum. Now it was August, and David and Mal were determined to make the best of the time before they had to go back to school the following month, when they would be starting secondary.

The adventure started on a Tuesday evening. Eleven-year olds don't normally believe in spooky things, but after that evening, David did begin to wonder. He had had his supper and his dad said it was OK for him to take a walk in the park with Luna, and so he set off quite happily, humming to himself as he went, his mobile phone in his pocket. He walked across the grass out the back of the house and made his way towards the brook. The trees were in full leaf and some large branches had fallen to the ground, probably because of the recent strong winds. The hollow oak to the left of the bridge over the brook had ivy curling around it.

This reminded David of the serpents he had read about in a book he had just finished. He crossed the bridge over the brook and then started to walk across the grass towards the woods. It had been a bright sunny day but now the sun had gone in, and although it was not yet dusk it felt as though the light was fading.

Luna and David ran and walked for a while, and then David, feeling tired, decided to sit and get his breath back. He found a comfortable-looking piece of grass and sat down facing the woods. Luna sat for a moment too and then began walking around despondently, waiting for them to be on the move again. David looked towards the woods. He then saw a large black dog, perhaps a Labrador, run out of the woods. It ran around briefly and then disappeared back amongst the trees. David sat for a while longer and watched as it ran in and out of the trees several times. There appeared to be no-one with the dog and David thought it was rather strange. The dog did not appear to be 'happy' and David began to get a strange feeling that something was not quite right. That someone or something needed help.

After having sat for a while David decided to walk over towards the trees to see what was going on. With Luna by his side he made his way across. As he got nearer to the woods, he saw the dog again. He then heard a voice, a boy's voice, perhaps, calling out. He could not make out the words but presumed it was the dog's name. David then saw a flash of colour as if someone was running through the trees. He then saw more colour off to the right. The voice continued and this time there was an additional sound that David could hear, but it seemed to come from within his own head. It was as if someone was asking him for help. David felt a shiver of fear. This was not someone out just walking their dog. Something odd was going on.

He stood for a moment longer then ran quickly up to the trees to see if he could see anything. He saw the dog once more but no humans, though the strange calling and feeling that he had continued. Feeling spooked, David turned around and together with Luna they started to run back towards the brook. He turned once to look again, and he was surprised to see the dog standing still with two small people. He blinked for just half a second, but when he looked again there was nothing. It was just as if the three of them had vanished into thin air. David noticed Luna's hackles go up and she gave out a low growl as he blinked again. Then the two of them sped back to the bridge and back home.

It was a strange evening. David thought of calling Mal, but they were due to meet the following morning and so instead he just pondered silently on what he had seen, and later in the evening he made his way up to bed thinking it would be a good idea to investigate again the next day. He found it difficult to settle, but eventually his tiredness got the better of him.

As he fell deeper and deeper into sleep, David found himself walking towards the woods with Luna by his side. He knew he was looking for something, but his thoughts were hazy and his mind unclear. Soon they both reached the woods. All around them were trees in their summer clothing. A proliferation of leaves. Oak trees, silver birch and hornbeam were the ones he could name. On the ground bordering the pathway were giant ferns and masses and masses of stinging nettles and brambles. There was no-one about. The woods were quiet as the sun started to fade at the end of the day. A number of squirrels could be seen running across the undergrowth and climbing trees. David thought he knew the path he was following quite well. He decided it was safer to stick to a known path and remembered that eventually he should come to a clearing which he and Mal often spent time in.

David and Luna walked on and on and on and on. David was sure he should have reached the clearing by now, but it was strange. They seemed to be passing the same trees and undergrowth again and again. It was almost as if they were going around in circles, instead of walking a straight, just gently curving path. There was no sign of a dog or indeed anyone. David was not afraid. He had Luna by his side.

Suddenly, ahead of him, David saw the beginning of the clearing. What was left of the sun was shining down and creating a warm, welcoming carpet on the ground. As he reached the clearing he stopped. Luna nuzzled his hand and then he looked across the clearing and standing there was the black dog and two small people. They were looking across at him and then suddenly they dissolved into dust as if they had never been there.

At that point the light began to fade, and David noticed a chill in the air he had not been aware of earlier. A shiver ran down his spine. He felt cold. The sky moved swiftly towards darkness and he could no longer see across the clearing. A faint, but growing louder, musical sound began to rise from the clearing and all around was dark. When all was pitch-black a small light began to grow from across the clearing and faint shadows showed themselves. The dog and the two small people were just discernible, but this time there was a shadow visible of a taller person as well. Instead of feeling afraid, now David felt sure that the people he could see were in fact friendly but a little frightened and in need of help. David wanted to call out, but suddenly there was a tremendous flash of light and then nothing. Nothing at all.

The next thing David knew he was waking up in his own bed and the summer sun was streaming through the gap in his bedroom curtains. He looked at his mobile by his bedside and he saw the time, eight o'clock. He breathed deeply for a moment to clear his head and then grabbed his camouflage dressing gown from where he had left it on the floor and made his way down for breakfast.

David's mum looked up when he entered the kitchen. She was tidying up after having eaten her own breakfast. 'David, are you OK?' she asked. 'You look a bit pale this morning.'

David smiled. 'I'm fine, Mum,' he replied. 'It is just that I didn't sleep too well last night.'

'Oh, OK,' was the reply. 'Let's get on with washing our hands and testing your blood then. I am sure you will want to get your breakfast and your injection out of the way so that you will have a chance to be ready for when Mal calls for you later.'

David nodded, and the morning routine followed in the same pattern as any other morning since he had learned he had diabetes. It was his new way of life.

THREE

Mal arrived just after eleven o'clock. He looked a bit flustered. Apparently, his dad had had to work very late the previous evening. There had been a disturbance which he had, with another policeman, to take control of. He had hurt his arm, although not badly. His mum had been concerned because he had come home particularly late and was both tired and irritable when he did arrive. Everything seemed better in the morning, though, when his dad went back to work. Mal had a lot to talk about and so David did not really say anything about his experience the previous evening or his dream.

As the weather was quite good, the boys decided it would be great to go off into the woods with a drink and some sandwiches. David's mum put the lunch together for them and reminded them that David needed to eat at one o'clock or shortly afterwards. They then packed their rucksacks. It was decided they would go on foot and take Luna with them. As they left the house, they saw Aylea in her front garden. She was helping her mum tidy up some rubbish which presumably a fox had distributed across their lawn. Aylea lived with just her mum, and her mum had not been all that well lately. They chatted for a moment. Aylea always looked pleased to see David and Mal.

They duly set off, made their way across the brook and then walked across the grass. It was only then that David thought to mention the previous evening's events, although he did not mention his dream. Mal's interest was aroused and the boys duly decided that they would conduct a search to see what they could find. Luna walked along happily with them, occasionally running ahead or sniffing something along the way.

Strangely there were not many people about. The day had started with sunshine, but it was beginning to cloud over and although rain was not due the wind began to blow. As they entered the woods the trees were swaying in the strong breeze and there was the sound of the rustling of many leaves. There was no other sound and as they walked further into the woods, a blanket of quiet descended on them.

They came to a favourite clearing. Three large dead trees stood in the space. They all had large trunks which were hollow in many places and presumably home to many insects and birds. A few brave twigs remained, reaching their dead fingers out to the sky and the surrounding woods. The boys saw an old man walking his spaniel but no-one else, which was a little unusual. After a while they decided that it was time to make camp and find somewhere good to sit and break out the sandwiches. They walked around until they found a really secluded spot away from the path they had been following. The three of them sat down. David poured some water for Luna and then the boys sat quietly munching their food and drinking.

Suddenly the boys became aware of the sound of running feet. This, they thought, was a little strange. They did not move from where they were seated but sat quietly listening. Two boys, a few years old than them, almost followed the path they had taken to find somewhere quiet to sit but turned to their right just before reaching them. They were carrying a bag and sat down with breathless thumps. They spoke quietly in gasps. David and Mal listened and held their breath. Luna sat quietly with David's hand on her head.

'We almost got caught this time,' one of the boys said.

'It would have been horrific to be caught with the stuff on us,' the other boy replied.

'What we gonna do?' the first boy said.

'Well, I reckon we ought to leave the bag here hidden. We can always come back for it tomorrow.'

'I guess you're right,' was the reply.

There was then the sound of hands scrabbling through the undergrowth. The boys then stood up and proceeded to walk further into the woods. They moved at a much slower pace than when they had arrived, presumably happy to be relieved of their burden.

David and Mal sat quietly until the older boys were well out of sight. They passed knowing looks between them but did not speak until all was quiet again.

David spoke first. 'Wow, Mal, I think we have just been in the company of a couple of villains. I wonder what on earth they stole and who did they steal it from and where did they steal it?'

'Lots of questions, David,' Mal replied, 'but let's go and see what they buried.'

The boys packed up the remnants of their lunch and made their way with Luna to where the older boys had sat. Both of them hunted around in the undergrowth and Luna joined in the hunt. After a couple of minutes Mal found the bag that had been hidden. It was a largish bag with a distinctive blue badge, and it was fairly heavy and looked like it could belong to either a man or a woman.

'Wow,' said David, quite taken aback to find the stolen goods. 'What do you think we should do, Mal?'

'We must take it to the police station,' Mal replied. 'My dad is a sergeant and that is what he would want us to do. The bag can then be returned to its owner.'

'You're right,' replied David, 'but if we walk back home with it someone may think we stole it, so why don't we take a photo of it and send a family WhatsApp to show everyone what we have found? We can then pack the bag inside one of our rucksacks so that it is out of sight.'

Mal nodded and took out his phone. 'Good idea, David.'

Unfortunately, Mal did not have a signal, but David did, and so the plan was put into action and soon the boys were making their way to the edge of the woods and back home. Because of what had happened and the situation they now found themselves in, they both forgot about their search for the black dog and the two small people David had seen the day before. However, just before they reached the edge of the trees, they heard barking off to their right. As they looked across, they saw, some distance from them, a black dog and one small person, probably a boy about their own age. Just as soon as they saw them a voice called out and both the dog and the boy disappeared out of sight. There was no further sound other the wind blowing in the trees and their feet upon the footpath. David knew without doubt that the dog and the child were the ones he had seen the previous evening, but there was no time to stop. They hurried on, and soon they were out of the woods and making their way across the grass towards the bridge over the brook, well on their way back to David's house. The stolen bag safely stowed in Mal's rucksack.

As they hurried out into their road they looked down to David's house and to their surprise they saw an ambulance parked at the roadside. They quickened their pace, anxious to see what had happened. As they drew closer, they saw that the vehicle was, in fact, parked directly outside Aylea's house. Standing in the front garden was David's mum with Aylea, who was looking very pale and tearful.

'What's happened?' David called out. 'Where's your mum, Aylea?'

David's mum called to him to speak quietly and then started to explain. Aylea's mum, Susan, had fallen down the stairs, banging her head and hurting her arm. As she was dazed Aylea had phoned David's mum, who had taken one look and decided the best thing to do was to phone for an ambulance. The paramedics who had arrived had recommended that a visit to the hospital was the most sensible course of action. At the moment another neighbour,

Pam, was helping put a bag together for Susan to take with her. Pam had also agreed to accompany Susan to the hospital whilst Aylea would stay with David's mum, who would look after her for as long as necessary. Aylea looked very worried and the boys did their best to reassure her.

After about ten minutes or so, Susan and the neighbour were safely stowed in the ambulance and the house made secure. Aylea kissed her mum goodbye and then David and the others watched the ambulance drive off before making their way into the house.

David's mum was a little shaken. 'What an eventful afternoon,' she said. 'First of all, Susan's tumble and then the excitement of your adventure in the woods.' She then turned her attention to Aylea. 'Come along, Aylea,' she said kindly. 'Let's go into the kitchen and get ourselves and the boys a drink. We can then sit down and decide what to do next.' Aylea followed David's mum quietly into the kitchen.

They had all been seated in the lounge for just a short while, with the boys and David's mum doing their best to reassure Aylea, when the doorbell rang. Looking out of the window they were surprised to see a police car, and when the front door was opened there was Mal's dad in uniform with another man in plain clothes.

'Hello, John,' said David's mum in surprise. 'Would you like to come in?'

'Yes, please, Viv,' was the reply, 'and may I introduce my colleague, Detective Chief Inspector Miles.'

David's mum escorted them through to the lounge, where she offered them each a seat. They declined the offer of tea, looking keen to explain the reason for their visit.

John looked across to Mal and David. 'I received your message,' he said, 'and the photograph of what you discovered in the woods. Do you have the bag with you now?'

'Yes, of course, Dad,' Mal replied. He then reached for his rucksack on the floor and passed it to his dad. John proceeded to open it up and took the bag out, which he then passed to his colleague.

The DCI then looked across at David and Mal and asked, 'Have you opened the bag and looked inside, lads?'

'No,' replied David. 'Our main concern, once we had found it, was to get back home safely with it so that it could be returned to its owner.'

'Excellent,' replied the DCI. 'You see, we suspect that the contents of this bag could possibly be something pretty important that we are trying to find. Fortunately, when your dad received your message, he recognised it and then brought it to my attention.'

The inspector then looked inside the bag, without making the contents visible to the others. He nodded and then turned to Mal's dad. 'Well done, Sergeant,' he said. 'Yes, this is it. Good news indeed.'

The DCI then explained that it was important now for him to take the bag back to the police station to keep it secure until it could be collected. 'It would be very useful, though,' he said, 'if we could talk to the boys who hid it in the woods. They may be able to provide some very useful information.'

David and Mal looked at each other with surprised looks on their faces. They were both beginning to realise that what they thought was a simple bag snatch in the high street was turning out to be something much more interesting and exciting.

The DCI then enquired, 'Did you get a good look at the boys, when all this happened?'

David and Mal exchanged glances. David spoke. 'Well, not really, sir. The most we actually saw of them was when they were walking away from where they had hidden the bag. We could see they were both taller and older than us. We probably wouldn't recognise them if we saw them out in the street, but I think it is likely if we saw them walking around the woods, we might recognise them.'

'Right,' said the DCI. 'We know from what you have said that the boys were planning to return tomorrow to collect the bag. So, what we need to do is put under surveillance the area where they believe the bag is still hidden. We need to do this as soon as possible, as they may decide to come back before tomorrow, even possibly in the night. We will remove the contents of the bag and take them to safety at the station. We can then use the bag as bait. We will fill it so that it looks and weighs much the same as it did today. When the boys return and find the bag, we will then be in a position to apprehend them and hopefully learn more from them about how they came by it. We will need the help, though, of you two boys if you are happy to be of assistance. We will need you to show us where in the woods the bag was buried. We will then be in a position to provide manpower to intervene when the boys return for it.'

Everyone was silent for a moment, thinking about what the DCI had said. Mal then spoke. 'I am happy to go back to where we found the bag if that will help. I can go now if you want.' David nodded in agreement.

David's mum then spoke. 'David, it might be just as well if you let Mal go and you stay here. There has been a lot going on for you today and we need to think about your diabetes. We will need to check your blood sugar within the next hour and you might not be back in time.'

David smiled. 'OK, you are right, Mum, and in any case one of us needs to stay here with you and Aylea.' He was aware that despite all the excitement about the bag, Aylea was still very pale and obviously very concerned about her mum.

'That's settled then,' said John. He looked at the inspector. 'Would you like me to change into plain clothes, sir, and then set off with Mal to replace the bag and mark surveillance for our people?'

'Yes, Sergeant. Good idea. Report back to me with your location when you have completed the task and, in the meantime, I will hasten to organise officers for a stakeout until the task is complete.'

With a plan now in place, they started to put it into action. The DCI went to a quiet corner of the room with the bag and emptied the contents into an evidence sack he withdrew from his pocket. He then passed the empty bag to John, who, together with David's mum, filled it with some suitable items they found in the kitchen. 'If you would like to wait here, Mal,' he said, 'I will go back to the house and change and then we can set off.'

'OK, Dad,' Mal replied. 'See you shortly then.'

David then asked a question. 'Can I ask, please? Are you able to tell us what all this is about?'

'I am sorry, young man,' the DCI replied. 'As much as I would like to, I am afraid I am not at liberty to say.'

David nodded. It was the answer he and Mal had expected.

The DCI and John then exchanged a few ideas before the DCI picked up the evidence bag containing the stolen goods, thanked everyone for their help and then made his way to the front door to drive back to the police station. Shortly afterwards John set off home to change out of his uniform.

David's mum asked Mal if he wanted anything to eat before setting off back to the woods. It was decided to put together a couple of drinks and snacks for him and his dad to take back with them in case they had to wait more than a short while before they were relieved.

A quarter of an hour later John returned. Both he and Mal were impatient to be off and so they said hasty goodbyes to the others with a promise to return later to confirm that they were OK and that everything was in place.

FOUR

With just the three of them left in the lounge, David's mum asked Aylea to explain again in more detail quite what had happened to her mum. Aylea explained that her mum had not been feeling very well for a few weeks. She knew that she had been down to the doctors but didn't quite know what it was all about. Aylea then explained that her mum had seemed very tired all day and then when she was making her way downstairs, she had tripped and fallen to the bottom. Fortunately, she had only been halfway down the stairs when she had fallen. She had knocked her arm badly as she tried to save herself. Had then slipped further down, banging her head on the way. Aylea had seen all this as she was walking down the stairs behind her at the time. When her mum had failed to get up or speak clearly, Aylea had grabbed her phone, which was in her pocket, and phoned David's mum for help.

'I am so glad that you did,' David's mum exclaimed at the end of Aylea's explanation. 'We now have to wait, though, until we hear on the phone from your mum or Pam at the hospital. Until then you are safe with us.'

By this time, it was getting on for four o'clock. 'It has been such a strange day so far,' David's mum said. 'And do you know, when I went down to the vegetable patch at the end of the garden this morning, I found that someone seems to have taken some of our tomatoes, lettuce and fruit. That has never happened before. Someone must have climbed over the back fence from the park, presumably when it was dark. It definitely was not birds or a fox.'

'That really is strange,' said David. 'I wonder who it was.' Something stirred in his memory at that point but only for a second, as his mum then suggested they might like to watch a movie as there was not much they could do for the time being. They opted for *Trolls World Tour*, and David and Aylea settled down to watch whilst David's mum went to clear up in the kitchen.

By the time the movie had finished, Aylea was beginning to get very anxious about her mum. Shortly afterwards, there was a call from Pam. She confirmed that Susan was with the doctor in A&E. Whilst she was still in some pain, she was speaking more clearly and was quite concerned about Aylea. David's mum asked Pam to reassure Susan that Aylea was absolutely fine and that as she would be preparing dinner shortly, she would, of course, be quite happy to cook for Aylea as well. Pam sounded pleased to hear this news. David's mum went on to say that, if necessary, it would be quite OK for Aylea to stay the night in the spare room. Pam said she would relay all this information back to Susan and would ring again when she had more news. David's mum asked Pam if she was OK to stay at the hospital for the time being. Pam said it was fine. As her husband was away on business at present it was not a problem.

After the phone call from Pam everyone felt a little more relaxed and David's mum set about planning the evening meal. David's dad was expected about six o'clock and they would eat shortly after that. As it would be a while before the meal was ready David and Aylea took Luna for a short walk. On the way back they met Mal and John. They had been to the woods and deposited the bag back where it had been found earlier. They had waited until officers had arrived to cover the stakeout overnight. Everything had gone quite smoothly, and they had not seen anyone else in the woods other than a lady walking her dog. Mal enquired after Aylea's mum and then he and his dad returned to their own house for the rest of the evening. Mal and David agreed to FaceTime before bed.

Back home again, the evening consisted of eating, testing blood sugar and David's regular insulin injection. David's dad listened with interest to all that had taken place that day. Pam phoned around seven o'clock and reported that it had been decided to keep Susan in overnight as they wanted to keep an eye on her and also do some tests. It was agreed that Aylea would stay overnight at David's, and David's dad said he would ensure that Aylea got to see her mum the next day if she had to stay in hospital longer or he would collect and bring her home, whichever was required. By 8.30pm David and Mal had spoken and agreed to meet the next day. It was time to go to bed. David's mum made sure Aylea had everything she needed. David duly said goodnight and made his way up to bed, tired but intrigued as to what tomorrow would bring.

There was much running through David's mind as his head sunk into his pillow. Tomorrow promised to be interesting as he hoped to learn more about the mystery of the stolen bag and to hear good news about Aylea's mum. However, when his eyes finally closed and he sank into deep sleep it was to his dream from the night before that he returned.

FIVE

Once again, David was standing on the edge of the clearing in the woods with Luna by his side. There was startling brightness all around him. His eyes felt totally drawn to what he could see on the other side of the clearing. One boy stood on his own. A little distance away stood another smaller boy and the black dog, but they were slowly walking away into the trees, leaving the older boy on his own. David started to walk cautiously across the clearing. He wanted to speak, but the words would not come. As he got nearer to the boy, he reached out to him and when he was within a few feet the boy reached out to him.

Before their fingertips even touched, there was an earth-shuddering flash of brilliance, and David felt himself melting and merging into the other boy. He blinked and realised in one mind-numbing moment that he had become one with the boy whilst retaining his own identity. He knew in a split second that the boy was called Daniel, that he was twelve years old, that he had a brother called Jake who was nine years old and that his mother was called Lisa. David, with his new eyes, looked back across the clearing and saw himself and Luna on the other side. He blinked again and the David he saw with his dog gradually faded until their shadows disappeared completely.

The boy Daniel stood silent for a moment and then followed the path the other boy and the dog had taken into the trees. He hurried to catch them up and before long the three of them were walking along together in companionable silence. To begin with there was a clear path, but gradually it disappeared, the woodland became more dense and their journey then took them along a very narrow track with a thick undergrowth of brambles, ferns and creeping ivy on either side. Occasionally a small animal scurried by in the undergrowth. No words were spoken as they hurried to their destination. The light began to fade. Daniel was leading the group and after a while he gently urged Jake to increase his pace.

After what seemed an age, the two children and the dog stepped from a densely wooded area into a small breathing space where no trees grew and there was a break in the brambles. The space was just large enough to accommodate a blue ridge tent, outside of which there was a camping chair and a couple of boxes. Someone could be seen moving around inside the tent.

Daniel called out, 'Mum, we're back.'

Hurried movement from within the tent resulted in 'Mum' emerging. She was small in stature, wore dark blue denim trousers and a long, baggy blue sweater. Mum's face wore a worried frown. Her face looked puffy and her hair was awry.

'Where have you been, boys?' she asked. 'I was really beginning to worry about you.'

Daniel apologised, 'Sorry, Mum, we just walked further than we meant to, but we're back now.'

Mum proceeded to spread a sheet on the ground. She then brought out some sandwiches for them all and some food for the dog, which was called Baz. The food was welcome if plain. The drink that followed was simply water, refreshing although warm.

'When can we leave the woods?' asked Jake. 'I so want to sleep in a proper bed and to see my friends.'

'It won't be long now,' said Mum. 'You know we have to wait a while, then everything will be OK.'

'Are you sure it will be OK?' replied Jake.

'Yes,' said Mum. 'I will make sure it will be.' She spoke with determination but looked unsure and slightly worried. Daniel noticed, but Jake just listened to her words and seemed reassured by them.

For just a short moment David was able to break free of Daniel and see him, his brother and their mum more clearly. What he saw concerned him. He saw three people who looked very alone and yes… frightened. They seemed to have lost their way and needed help. David so wanted to help, and he so wanted to speak and understand. He tried to concentrate his thoughts as to how he could possibly help. Concentrating made his head spin and he suddenly began to wonder where Luna was. He looked up and there she was quite clearly. No-one else seemed to be able to see her.

David suddenly knew that it was time for him to go, although he did not want to. He separated from the little

29

group without being able to say goodbye and walked towards Luna. When he reached her and placed his hand on her back the world spun into a myriad of silver stars, and the next thing he knew, he was waking up in his bed at home with Luna on the floor beside him and the sun shining brightly through his bedroom window. He checked his phone by the side of his bed. He saw that it was eight o'clock and that there was a WhatsApp from Mal.

After a minute or two David felt fully awake. He remembered his dream quite clearly and knew without any doubt whatsoever that he had to find Daniel and his small family and help them. He also knew that he could not do it alone and that he would need the help not only of Mal and Luna but also a grownup, his own dad or Mal's dad.

He reached for his phone and read Mal's message. 'I'll be round about nine o'clock. I had such a weird dream last night. See you later. Mal.'

At the breakfast table Aylea was looking worried and David's mum was doing her best to calm her down and reassure her.

'You remember, Aylea,' she said, 'the doctor will finish his rounds at the hospital before noon and once that has happened, we will know more. If your mum is not able to come home today, we will take you to visit her this afternoon. So, do try not to worry.'

David's mum helped him check his blood and do his injection. Breakfast and bathroom took up the rest of the time until a knock on the door let them know that Mal had arrived.

Mal had an odd look on his face as he sat down with a plonk on the sofa. 'I hardly slept at all last night,' he said, 'but when I did, I had such a strange dream. I normally forget my dreams, but this one is quite clear in my memory.'

'I had a weird dream too, Mal,' replied David, 'but tell us about yours first.'

Mal was clearly spooked. He had dreamt that the bag in the woods contained plans by a far eastern power to create and release a deadly virus, more lethal than even Covid-19.

'Oh, Mal,' said David's mum. 'What a horrible, horrible dream. You have such a vivid imagination. I can understand why you look so disturbed by your dream. But it was just a dream, Mal. So, try to put it out of your mind. Such a possibility is too horrific to dwell upon.'

Mal produced a crooked smile. He then remembered Aylea's worries, turned to her and said, 'Sorry, Aylea. How are you feeling this morning? Everything will be alright, y'know.'

She smiled back at him. 'Oh, Mal, I really hope so!' she said.

Mal then turned to David. 'So, what did you dream about, David? Did you dream about the contents of the bag? Oh, don't tell me you had the same dream as me. Please don't tell me that.'

'No,' replied David. 'It was a very different dream.' He then slowly and carefully explained to everyone about his first encounter with the two boys and the black dog at the edge of the woods two days ago. He then went on to speak about what had occurred in his dream and how worried he felt that the people he had seen were at risk and needed help. He turned to his mum. 'I am sorry, Mum, I know this must sound very strange, but I don't think it was just a dream. I

31

believe I know where to find them. It is nowhere near where the bag was buried.'

David's mum looked perplexed. Everyone sat quiet for a moment without speaking. Even Aylea's face lost its worried look as she tried to puzzle out what David had said.

David's dad, who had sat quietly throughout, then spoke. 'David, I can see how concerned you are. I think the only and best thing we can do is take a walk into the woods before lunch and have a look. Mal can come with us with Luna whilst Aylea can stay here with Mum and wait for news from the hospital.'

'Yes, please,' replied David. 'I think that is a really good idea, Dad. Thanks. Good thing it is your day off today, isn't it!'

'We must take some provisions with us,' said David's dad, entering into the spirit of adventure. 'Yes,' he said. 'I know David has to eat at one o'clock latest so I will make allowance for that in case it takes longer than it should. It is only just past nine o'clock now, so if we make haste, we could well be back home in plenty of time for lunch.'

Just before they left David's mum asked, 'Mal, is your dad working today?'

'Yes,' said Mal. 'He is on standby at the moment but will move to the stakeout, if necessary, by four o'clock.'

Goodbyes said and mobile phones stowed, as well as provisions of food and water, the three then set off on their quest. Mal felt quite caught up in the preparations and almost forgot about his dream. The early sun had given way to an overcast sky as they made their way over the bridge onto the grass beyond. It did not look like rain, though, so the three, together with Luna, set off happily at a steady pace towards the woods. Once they reached the woods David led them confidently down a path that Mal also knew. It was, as David said earlier, in a different direction to where the mystery bag was hidden.

The path the three followed took them deeper into the wood. They walked on and on until they came to a clearing. This was one both he and Mal knew and the clearing David had seen in his dream. He led them across to the other side and he then, without knowing why or how, knew exactly which way to walk, to follow the path he had taken in his dream. They made their way down the long, narrow path with dense brambles on either side with the wood closing in on them.

SIX

Daniel had awoken early that morning feeling worried. He felt that although he was only twelve, as the oldest male there at their campsite, it was his job to look after his mum and his brother. They had been in the woods for two days now and he didn't really like it. He knew that in 2021 people did camp in the woods, but he didn't feel safe and he was aware that they didn't have too much food left. He felt positively bad about climbing the fence the night before last and stealing the vegetables from the garden, but he just wanted to help his mum out. He knew she was worried and unsure. Jake seemed reasonably OK. For him this was just a big adventure. Well, it was for Daniel too to begin with, but no longer. Baz helped them to feel safe, but Daniel really wanted to see his friends again and he was even looking forward to going back to school, which was unusual for him.

He had awoken before the others that morning and sat outside the tent for a while, mulling things over. He thought he should have a plan, but after a while he realised that he simply didn't have one. After the other two had woken up and they had eaten a sparse breakfast Daniel suggested that he, Jake and Baz take a walk around the woods. He felt that walking would help him think. They duly set off on the route Daniel knew best. He hummed quietly to himself, mainly to keep his spirits up, although he knew his mum had told them not to draw attention to themselves. Both the boys were wearing shorts and Jake unfortunately stumbled and caught his leg against some brambles. He let out a yelp and Daniel couldn't help himself saying, 'Shush.' He then washed Jake's leg with some water he was carrying in a bottle.

A few minutes further on Daniel came to a sudden halt and held his hand up to Jake to keep quiet. Baz also froze in his tracks as if sensing the importance of staying still. Ahead of him and coming towards them down the pathway was a very tall black man; accompanying him were two boys who looked a little younger than himself and a German shepherd dog. Even though they had been careful Daniel realised that they had been spotted. He felt rooted to the spot as the three people walked up to them with their dog.

Something very strange happened then. The three stood still as if in surprise, their dog holding back also, then one of the boys stepped forward and held out his hand as he spoke. 'Hello, Daniel,' said the boy. 'My name is David and we have come to help you and Jake and your mum.'

Daniel was stunned. He did not know this boy or the other boy or the tall man walking with him, but, somehow, he knew their names. He felt spooked, but at the same time there was something in the back of his mind that told him everything was alright. What he did not realise then was that the man and the boy accompanying David were as spooked as Daniel was. They were, of course, aware of his dream the night before.

Daniel simply did not know what to say and neither did Jake, who moved closer to his brother. David's dad at that point felt it was up to him to speak.

'Daniel, we do not really know what is going on, but David here seems to think you might need some sort of assistance. My name is Mr Robert Williams, this is my son, David, and my nephew, Mal. We live on the other side of the brook. I believe you are in the woods here with your mother. Would you like to take us to meet her?'

Daniel still felt unable to speak but also felt that he had to do something so thought what would be for the best. He gathered his thoughts. 'Yes, OK, sir,' he replied. 'If you follow me and Jake, we will take you to our tent. It is not too far, but when we get close please let me go ahead and speak to Mum so that she is prepared.'

Everyone agreed to the plan and so Daniel set off back the way he had come with his brother and the others following.

Before too long Daniel lifted his right hand to indicate that they had arrived. Having signalled to the others to wait, he went forward to speak to Lisa, his mum. He found her sitting despondently outside the tent with a sad, blank look on her face. Daniel went up to her and, crouching down to be level with her face, he explained what had happened and that they had visitors. Lisa looked worried and a little frightened, so Daniel put his hand on her arm to reassure her.

'Two of them are black,' Daniel said, 'and they seem very nice.'

SEVEN

Lisa was unsure. She didn't know what to think but decided that it would be good to talk to the visitors. *Surely,* she thought, *it couldn't do any harm.* She nodded to Daniel, who then called to the others to come forward. Lisa stood up and saw a very tall man accompanied by two boys approaching. She also saw their German shepherd, who seemed to be fine with Baz.

'Hello,' ventured Lisa. 'I don't understand. How did you know we were camping in the woods and how did you know where to find us?'

David's dad stepped forward and introduced himself, David and Mal. He then tried to explain how they knew where to find them and their camp, but he didn't really have a clear explanation to offer.

The conversation was becoming rather muddled when he came to the main purpose of their visit. He tentatively asked, 'Please excuse me, but the general feeling is that you might need some help. So, do let us know if we can help because we would be only too pleased to do so? Please do not feel nervous about us. Mal's dad is a local police sergeant. I am not in the police, I work as an accountant, and my wife, who perhaps you might meet later, works as a volunteer.'

Lisa did not feel that she wanted to go into too much detail with the children around them, so after a few minutes she suggested that the boys take Luna for a walk for ten minutes or so, so that David's dad and she could talk. Baz would stay with them. David looked disappointed, but Daniel offered to take them to another interesting clearing a few minutes away, and so off they went, promising to be back shortly.

Lisa and Robert sat down on the groundsheet together. Lisa was surprised at herself. She did not feel afraid. She then started to explain what had happened and why she was living in the woods with her two sons and their dog, Baz.

'Everything was fine at home until the beginning of 2020. My husband, me and the boys, we were happy, so happy. Then Sam caught Covid-19. He was quite ill with it but fortunately the rest of us didn't get infected. Sam was in hospital for a week, not on a ventilator, though. He then came home. He slowly recovered but was never quite the same person as before. He'd been in the same job for five years, working in aviation, but he was laid off. He managed to find another job, but it was not so well paid. He then started to get into what I felt was bad company, and I was really not quite sure what he was up to, but I knew it was not good. A few times a strange man would call at the house. I was frightened for Sam and for the boys. I asked him to stop whatever he had got involved in, but he wouldn't. He then became aggressive and angry a lot of the time. I told him that things had to change.

'It all came to a head last Friday. It got so bad I said I was going to stay with my sister. I upped and packed bags for me and the boys, and put the tent in the boot of the car as well. However, after I left the house and phoned my sister, I learned that she had gone away on an impromptu holiday and I was not able to reach her, and so I simply came here to the woods with the tent and we have been here ever since. We have been using the carpark facilities over the back. I know we are not the only people doing this sort of thing in 2021. I know we can't stay here, and I have to do the best for the boys, but I really do not want to go home yet.' She paused for breath and looked across at Robert, who had sat quietly throughout Lisa's explanation.

'So does your husband have any idea where you are now?' asked Robert.

'I phoned to say we were fine and that we would be home after the weekend. I left it at that. I don't think he will be concerned because he seems so wrapped up in other things these days. I have tried to keep much of my worries from the boys. I think Daniel understands more, but Jake is a boy who does not worry much about things, which is all for the best really.'

Both Robert and Lisa paused for a moment, both thinking what to say next, when there came a shout and the four boys and Luna hurtled back into the clearing.

Daniel was the first to appear and he rushed up to the grownups. Breathlessly he explained, 'Something odd is going on, Mum. We heard shouting and people running. It really startled us. David seemed to think it could be something to do with something called a stakeout in another part of the woods. Mal said his dad was a policeman and is involved. I don't like it at all. Can we go home?'

Robert and Lisa looked at the boys and then each other. Robert came to a decision. 'I really think, Lisa, that it is not safe for you and the boys to stay here. Can I suggest that we pick up everything and make our way to my house, get something to eat and then think of a plan?'

Lisa paused for a moment. She had only just met this man and the two boys, but she had a good feeling about them, and she knew she had to do something, so she said, 'Yes, OK. Thank you. I really think that would be for the best. Boys, start collecting up your things. Robert, could you help me with the tent, please?'

Everyone set to work with a will whilst the two dogs nosed around in the undergrowth. Soon everything was collected up and the group set off in what David and Daniel knew to be the right direction. Robert checked his watch. They should just be back home in time for the one o'clock deadline for David's lunch.

A return journey can often seem to take less time than the time taken to reach a destination, but even though they hurried the walk seemed a long one. Everyone was carrying something and so they could not walk as fast as they would have liked. Jake dropped his bundle at some point and the others waited while he retrieved it from the undergrowth. Eventually, however, they emerged from the trees onto the grass. There were several sighs of relief. They had not encountered anybody on their journey. They made their way towards the bridge over the brook and soon they were back at Robert and David's house. Rather than using his key,

Robert thought he would ring the bell and then he could introduce everyone as they walked in the door. He could have phoned ahead but somehow it did not seem practical whilst carrying a tent. He was really not quite sure what his wife would say, so he rang the bell and waited, feeling just slightly uneasy!

The door opened very quickly. Apparently, David's mum had been looking out of the front-room window and spotted them coming along the road.

'Hello,' she called out in welcome. Aylea was standing just behind her, looking surprised and a little confused. 'Do come in, everyone. Robert, I can see everyone is carrying something, so could you please put the tent and all the other bits and pieces safely in the conservatory so that we have more space in the house?'

Lisa smiled when she saw David's mum and Aylea. *It's good to see some girls after being with nobody but boys for a while*, she thought.

Introductions over, they all sat down and Robert checked the time. It was coming up to one o'clock and so it was decided that the next thing to do was to have lunch. They could talk about everything afterwards. Lisa looked uncomfortable but then offered to help David's mum in the kitchen, so the two stood up to set about their task, but not before David's mum had asked him how he was.

'I'm fine, Mum,' said David, 'but I think I have to warn you that there have been some strange goings-on this morning, but I don't quite know the full story yet.'

Everyone went quiet. 'How do you know that, young man?' asked his dad.

'Sorry, Dad,' was the reply. 'I just have a very strong feeling, that is all.'

Mal nodded, his dream of the night before jumping into his mind. Enough said, the girls set off to prepare lunch with Aylea in tow.

Almost as soon as the girls went into the kitchen the landline rang. David's mum rushed back out to answer it, gasping, 'I expect it is the hospital.' Sure enough, it was Susan from the hospital with the news that she was fit enough to return home later in the afternoon. She just needed to wait for her discharge summary, but everything would be done by four o'clock if someone was able to collect her. She also added that she would have to see her GP, but there was nothing that could not be sorted out.

David's mum assured Susan that she would be along to collect her at around 4.30pm and that she would bring Aylea with her. Aylea, hearing the phone call, had rushed into the lounge and had a few hurried but very welcome words with her mum before the phone call was ended and the girls returned to the kitchen to prepare lunch.

The girls hurriedly prepared sandwiches for everyone together with a large bowl of salad and another of crisps. There was also some apple pie which stretched to a small slice for everyone. The lunch was enjoyed by all and washed down with tea, coffee and squash.

After everyone had eaten Robert suggested that the boys and Aylea go into the garden for a while to give the grownups a chance to talk.

David agreed. 'OK,' he said. 'The boules and the table football are in the garden, so we can find something to do.'

David and Mal actually were both really wondering what was happening with the stakeout; they knew they were going to have to wait but that their patience would be rewarded eventually.

With just the three grownups alone in the lounge there was the chance to talk about the serious matters confronting Lisa and her family. It was interesting and useful in a way that David's mum and Lisa had realised that they had met before, when the boys were much younger, at coffee mornings. Lisa explained again that she had been worried enough about what was happening with her husband to leave home and, not being able to stay with her sister, had taken the big, perhaps unwise, decision to camp in the woods. The issues were talked over for a while until Robert eventually thought they needed to form a plan.

After thinking for a few moments he ventured, 'Lisa, do you think it might be a good idea for you and the boys to stay with us for a couple of days? During that time perhaps you could contact your husband and suggest meeting him somewhere neutral to discuss the way forward?'

Lisa paused for a moment. 'I think that would be really helpful,' she said. 'I am so, so grateful to you. I know that my sister will be back in a few days and we will definitely be able to stay with her then if necessary. I think it would be a good idea to meet and talk seriously with Sam, and I can hopefully arrange something for tomorrow.'

At this point Lisa went into the kitchen to phone Sam. She was only gone for a couple of minutes. She returned to the lounge with a perplexed look on her face. 'His phone is switched off, which is unusual, and we don't have a landline,' she said. 'So, I will try again later.'

Robert asked Lisa where she had left her car. She explained and it was arranged that Robert would drive her to get it later so that the tent could be stowed in the boot.

The afternoon seemed to pass fairly rapidly and soon David's mum and Aylea were getting ready to drive to the hospital to fetch Susan.

David was concerned and said to his mum, 'Please, let Aylea's mum know that we can help her if she needs help. You will, won't you, Mum?'

'Of course,' was the reply.

After they had left the house to make their way to the car David's dad asked, 'Why did you say that, David?'

David looked at his dad. 'Just had a feeling, that's all.'

EIGHT

About the same time as David's mum and Aylea set off for the hospital, two boys, Mike and Tom, were crossing the bridge over the brook on their way to the woods to find the bag they had left there the day before. They both felt uncomfortable and nervous about going but neither really wanted to admit that to the other. They really had no idea what was in the bag that they had stolen from the back of a car with the rear window open. Something did not feel right, and something felt definitely quite wrong. This was not just a bag snatch. The boys had only done this sort of thing twice before. It all had started as a bit of a dare. They had not been caught or even nearly caught before, but this time they felt they had been seen. There had been a shout and then they had run, hell for leather. They had got away, but they had felt really scared and each really wanted to say to the other, 'Never again! This has got to be the last time we do this.' So, with heavy footsteps they both trudged across the grass into the woods, retracing their steps back to where they had left the bag.

The woods were as quiet as they had been the day before. The only person they did see was a tall black man walking at the edge of the woods, but they thought nothing of it. The man looked deep in thought and certainly did not seem to take any notice of them. After about fifteen minutes or so they came to where they thought they had left the bag. Mike seemed fairly sure of the location and so it was agreed that Tom would keep a lookout whilst Mike poked around in the undergrowth to find what they were looking for.

After a couple of minutes Tom heard Mike say, 'Got it, Tom. Here it is, just where I thought it was.' After two seconds of silence, during which the boys each felt a mixture of triumph and relief, the peace they had felt in the woods was totally shattered by three men who seemed to come out of nowhere and walked quickly up to them, holding cards out in front of them. Mike and Tom were suddenly almost paralysed with fear. Neither of them felt able to speak or move, let alone make a run for it.

'Good afternoon, boys,' the tallest man said. 'I am Detective Chief Inspector Miles and this is DC Brown and DC Stirling. Our warrant cards. I am afraid we have to ask you some questions.' Both the boys' faces went pale and beads of sweat formed on Mike's forehead.

'What about, Officer?' he said. 'We haven't done anything wrong. We just came out for a walk and we happened to find this old bag which we saw someone leave here the other day.'

'Come, come now,' said DCI Miles. 'I will be quite straight with you. We have information which leads us to believe that yesterday afternoon you arrived in the woods with this bag and that you left it here with a plan to collect it today. We also understand that the bag and its contents are not actually yours and that you came by them in what was probably a dishonest way.' Tom seemed to shrink into himself as he heard these words, whereas Mike tried to stand his ground and give an air of confidence and bravado.'

Mike considered his answer then spoke. 'We found it just lying around. We did not steal it and anyway, it probably doesn't contain anything much. You can have it. We don't want it, do we, Tom?'

Tom shook his head vigorously.

As there was no-one around in the woods, the DCI felt it safe to continue. 'I have to be honest with you boys. As it happens the contents of this bag are, or rather were because they have been removed, of considerable value and it is of paramount importance that you tell us precisely how you came by it. We can do this here or you can accompany us to the station.'

If it were possible, Tom's face at this statement went even paler and even Mike's air of bravado started to slip away.

'Oh, please, we don't want to go the station. We don't want any trouble. Tom, shall we take them to where we found the bag?'

Tom nodded vigorously at this friend.

'Come along then, boys,' said the DCI. 'Let's be off.'

At that moment the tall black guy that the boys had seen earlier came walking through the trees towards them. 'Hello, Sergeant,' said the DCI. 'You have arrived at just the right time. You can accompany me and these two young men to where they found the bag. We will take the car. My two colleagues here are going off duty and are local, so I am sure they will be OK to walk home.'

The two DCs nodded their agreement.

At this point the DCI advised Mike and Tom that they would be in an unmarked car and so they need not worry on that account but that it was very important that they tell the truth.

The party set off to the edge of the woods. Once there the two DCs walked one way whilst the others headed in another to the police car parked close by. Once inside the car the DCI asked and made a note of the boys' names and the sergeant, Mal's dad, also introduced himself. The DCI then asked where he should drive to.

Mike replied, 'Acacia Road, just off the High Street, about halfway down. We'll point the exact spot out once we get there, won't we, Tom?'

'OK,' replied the DCI. 'I know where you mean. Thanks.' With that the DCI started the car and drove off.

When Mike pointed out the spot, halfway down the road as stated previously, the DCI parked the car and turned off the engine. 'OK, boys,' he said. 'Now please describe to us exactly what happened.'

Mike took a deep breath and spoke slowly and clearly as if weighing up carefully each word before uttering it.

'Well, it was like this. Tom and me, we was walking down the road yesterday morning. It was around 10.30am, I think. I can't be sure as neither of us had any reason to look to see what time it was. As we walked along, we saw in front of us a red Peugeot 208. Two men got out. One of them had his phone to his ear. He immediately finished the call and then, seeming in a mad panic, he urged his friend to hurry as fast as he could. He almost seemed to drag him across the road and into the block of flats opposite. We noticed that they were in such a hurry that one of the men threw some litter on the ground as he rushed along, as if he didn't have time to think. As we walked up to the car, we saw that one of the windows was still open and there was the bag. Sorry, but we thought that, just for a lark, we would lift it. Once we had it, we realised that someone might have seen us. We thought we heard a noise. We were so spooked that we simply ran for it and ended up in the woods. We didn't know what to do, so we hid the bag with a view to coming back today to find it. We had no idea what it was. Could have been anything. We simply didn't know.'

'OK,' said the DCI. 'Are either of you able to describe the men or give me any part of the registration number of the car?'

Tom spoke at this point. 'I noticed the registration number included the letters GAG as we walked towards the car because I thought that it was funny. I don't remember too clearly what the men looked like. They were both tall, one taller than the other and both wore denims. They were white and had short hair. I can't remember anything else.'

'Thank you, Tom. Do you have anything to add, Mike?' asked the DCI.

'No, not really, sir,' replied Mike, who gave the impression, as did Tom, that he was really trying to be helpful.

After pondering over what the boys had said for a moment, the DCI then said, 'Thanks, boys. All I need now from you is for you to come down to the station to make brief statements and give us details of your full names and addresses. You have helped us and so you will not be in any trouble and this will not be taken any further but, and there is a but, if you are ever involved in anything of this nature again I can assure you that there will be no leniency the second time. Am I quite clear?'

Mike and Tom looked at each other and both spoke at once to reassure the DCI and the sergeant that they would never ever be involved in anything like this again and… they both meant it. Without further discussion the DCI started the car and they set off for the police station.

NINE

Almost at the same moment as the boys arrived at the police station, David's mum was arriving at Aylea's house. It had taken a little longer than they had hoped to get the discharge papers and Susan's prescription, but once everything had been completed the three of them were pleased to get into the car to drive home. Susan looked pale and said very little. She hugged Aylea until Aylea was almost fighting for breath. They were both very pleased to see each other and David's mum saw the hint of a tear in Susan's eye.

Once back home, David's mum parked the car and helped Susan and Aylea into the house. Then the three of them sat down on the sofa and David's mum offered to make them a drink. She also managed to find some biscuits and all three of them enjoyed the refreshments.

Susan was very quiet. Once she had finished her tea, she drew breath and started to speak. 'I had some blood tests whilst I was at the hospital yesterday and they confirmed something that the doctor has suspected for some time. Apparently, I am diabetic and I will probably need to take a drug to help me manage it.' Susan looked worried and unsure.

David's mum stepped in to reassure her. 'Don't worry, Susan, I am sure you will, with help, be able to get the condition under control if you do the right things. Did you know that my David is diabetic and has been now for over two years?'

Susan looked startled. 'Oh no, of course I remember now. But he is so young. How does he manage?'

David's mum smiled. 'He is very sensible. He understands what he has to do to keep well and, of course, me and his dad help.'

Just then there was a knock at the door. David's mum got up to answer and there stood David.

'May I come in, Mum?' he said. 'I thought I might be able to help.'

'Yes, do come in, David,' she said.

David came into the lounge and looked at Susan. 'I just had a feeling,' he said, 'that I might be able to help.'

Susan looked puzzled. 'But you have helped already, David,' she said. 'Your mum has just reminded me you are diabetic, and I've just been diagnosed diabetic, so being told how well you manage has made me feel much more confident and in control.'

David smiled. 'I had a feeling. That's all,' he said, 'and that is why I came around.'

David's mum looked at her watch. 'Good heavens!' she said. 'Talking of the importance of regular meals, I must get back to the kitchen and start dinner.' She turned to Susan. 'I'll call by in the morning to see how you are, but if you need anything at all you know where we are, just next door.' With that she ushered David out of the door to hurry back home with the intention of getting into the kitchen to start the evening meal.

When David and his mum walked into the living room everyone was engaged in either chatting or looking at their phones. Luna and Baz were looking around at everyone wondering who was going to volunteer to take them for a walk. David's mum asked everyone how they were and she recounted briefly that Susan and Aylea were now home and all was well. She did not mention Susan's diabetes.

Lisa was looking a little anxious and so she asked her if she had managed to get Sam on his mobile yet. 'Not yet, I'm afraid, and I have called twice and left messages. All rather odd. I guess I will have to wait a little longer.'

'Dinner will be about an hour,' David's mum announced, 'so why don't some of you go out with Luna and Baz for a while? Lisa and I can manage here.'

'Good idea,' said David's dad. 'Come on, boys. Let's be off. I know, I'll get David back in good time to check his bloods.' With that he sprang up and the dogs looked relieved and eager to be off.

As the boys were putting their shoes on David's mum asked Mal if he would be staying for dinner. He replied that his mum was expecting him but that he would be back early the next day. Soon the four boys, Robert and the dogs were making their way to the bridge over the brook to take a walk and kick the ball around that David had brought with him.

David's mum and Lisa went into the kitchen. Checking that it would be fine for Lisa and her boys, David's mum started to prepare veggie curry and rice. This was one of Robert's favourites.

'I am sorry, Lisa. This must be really difficult for you, especially now Sam is not responding on his phone. Do you have any idea what the problem is?'

Lisa, who was perched on a high kitchen stool, thought for a moment. 'Sam just seemed to get so anxious. It was as if he was hiding something. He was never like that before. He was irritable, more with me than with the boys, really. Once or twice someone came around for him and they went off down the pub, but there was something I didn't like about the man. I can't say what, but I just knew it wasn't right and for me it couldn't continue. Life was beginning to get very difficult.'

'Don't worry, we will get to the bottom of it, I am sure,' said David's mum.

The two then continued to prepare the meal and reminisce about when they had met a few years back at the coffee mornings.

The evening passed fairly quickly after the meal. David's mum sorted out the sleeping arrangements with Lisa's help. There was general talk and David WhatsApped some of his school friends for a half hour or so on general things, steering carefully clear of anything to do with recent events as he and Mal had been asked to do. Lisa tried Sam again, but once more there was no response and she continued to look anxious. David was feeling rather tired and so he went to bed fairly early. The day had been a busy one, with the last part being lots of general chatter with Daniel and Jake.

TEN

David's head had not been on the pillow long when he fell deeply asleep. Gradually he became aware that he seemed to be walking down a long, pitch-black tunnel. He walked for quite a while before he saw any light at all. Once a glimmer of light appeared in the distance, it grew steadily as David's legs trudged forwards. Eventually he walked out of the tunnel and found himself in the High Street. He continued to walk forward, turning right into what he saw was Acacia Road. This was somewhere he had only been once before with his dad. His legs took him down the road until he saw a man, a tall man. He was standing in the middle of the pavement and gave no sign of moving, his phone clamped to his ear, a worried look on his face. David could not stop himself walking towards him, and as he drew nearer, he felt himself being pulled forward until he suddenly realised that he had walked into the man's mind.

It was not a comfortable place to be. Whilst there were feelings of love, for his family, and some happiness, there was also worry and fear. David could see dark images lurking in dark corners. There was a feeling of being trapped, unable to escape. A feeling almost of despair. David could not tell whether this was because of what the man was feeling emotionally or because of a difficult situation in which he found himself. David struggled as hard as he could to be released and eventually every part of him was exhausted with the effort. He felt so tired that he had almost given up, when he suddenly found himself back on the pavement with a jolt seeing the man again from just a few feet away. He had moved a little and was about to get into a red car. David felt sorry for the man, but at the same time he so wanted to get away from him. He turned around and walked as quickly as he could back in the direction of the High Street. As he drew closer everything went dark and then darker still. Eventually the vision was gone completely and he fell into a fathomless, dreamless sleep.

David did not dream for the rest of the night. When he awoke his dream was quite clear in his mind. Luna was lying by the side of his bed and looked up at him with knowing eyes as he put his feet to the floor ready to start the day. Luna sensed his concern and nuzzled David's hand.

Downstairs breakfast was in full swing. The usual procedure, specially for David, was carried out and his mum was slightly concerned as his blood sugar was a little higher than it should have been. Everyone seemed to be talking. David's dad was just off to work, but his mum was home all this week as she was having a few days' break from her volunteer work, which was just as well seeing as it was such a strange and eventful week. Lisa continued to look strained. After everyone had eaten, she went into the kitchen, where it was quieter, to try Sam's number again. Before long she returned, shaking her head as before. She looked really concerned now.

As Lisa sat down on the sofa David started to talk about his strange dream. His mum looked at him and, shaking her head, said, 'I don't know, David, not another dream. I am beginning to wonder what is going on.'

David recounted slowly and clearly what he had dreamt. No-one interrupted him, but as he spoke Lisa's face got paler and paler. Daniel and Jake just stared at David as if awestruck.

When David had finished speaking Lisa blurted out. 'But we live in Acacia Road and we have a red car. What is going on? I don't understand. I just don't understand.'

Before anyone had a chance to speak there was a ring on the doorbell and David's mum rose quickly to answer it. In came Mal and his dad, who had not long risen from bed after working the late shift. Everyone was quiet when they walked in. David's mum found a seat for Mal's dad whilst Mal happily sat down on the floor. Mal's dad was introduced to everyone. He had heard from Mal the day before about Lisa and her boys staying with David's family.

The new arrivals immediately sensed an atmosphere and Mal's dad asked, 'Is everything OK? You all look rather worried.'

David's mum then took it upon herself to explain about the difficulty Lisa was having trying to reach her husband, David's dream and Lisa's shock at hearing about the dream as she and her family live in Acacia Road and her husband has a red car.

Mal's dad then asked Lisa if his phone had a personal tracking app. She replied, 'No. I did ask him once to get one, but he said, no, he didn't want one.'

'That's a pity,' said Mal's dad. He thought for a moment. 'I would like to have a private word with you, Lisa, if I may?' He turned to David's mum and she quickly answered before he had to ask.

'You can both go into the kitchen if that would be suitable. You will have privacy there and I will make sure that you are not disturbed.'

David and Mal looked at each other in bewilderment whilst Daniel and Jake just looked worried. David's mum did her best to make light conversation about what the boys might do in the morning. Not much was said. No-one was trying to hear what was being said in the kitchen. They were just waiting.

Mal's dad closed the kitchen door and the two of them perched on kitchen stools. Mal's dad spoke first.

'As you know, Lisa, I am with the police, a sergeant. I've been in the force for six years now and it is an interesting life. I expect you will have heard from David and Mal that yesterday we staged a stakeout in the woods. We needed to apprehend the two boys who left a special bag in the woods the day before. I say special because the contents of the bag were top security. I am afraid I am not at liberty to say what the contents are. Indeed, I do not have too much detail myself. Well, our team waited and sure enough the two boys returned for the bag and so we were able to speak to them. What they eventually said, after encouragement, was that they had taken the bag from a red car in Acacia Road. Two men had got out of the car in a hurry and had accidentally left a window open. From what you have said I can only conclude that the car could well be your husband's. One of the boys remembered that the registration number contained the letters GAG. Would that then be your husband's car, Lisa?'

Lisa looked at him in shock. 'Yes, that is Sam's car. What on earth is going on?'

'I think the best thing we can do, Lisa,' said Mal's dad, 'is find him. I presume you don't have a landline, or you would have called it, so I think we had better try the house. Hopefully the boys can stay here. I am sure David's mum will look after them and give them lunch. Actually, I am not working at the moment as I don't start until later, but because of the importance of what is being investigated I think I had better phone the station first to ask how they would like to handle this.'

Lisa nodded.

'If you go and wait in the lounge I will phone through and then we can make a start. We can take my car.'

Everyone looked up as Lisa went back into the lounge. 'Don't worry, boys,' she said. 'Everything is OK. Mal's dad is just making a call through to his colleague and then he and I will go to find your dad.' She turned to David's mum. 'I am sorry, but will it be alright if the boys stay with you until this is all sorted out?'

David's mum nodded. 'No trouble at all, Lisa. We will plan something for the morning and then get ourselves some lunch. If you just keep in contact with us via phone that will be absolutely fine.'

'Thank you so much,' replied Lisa.

David looked and felt shocked, as did Mal, who was remembering his own dream from the night before last. Both tried, however, to put on a brave face for Daniel and Jake. Meanwhile David's mum did her best to give off an air of confidence and being in control. Everyone felt shaken at the turn of events.

Mal's dad then came back into the lounge. 'All good,' he said. 'We can set off now if you are ready, Lisa.'

She nodded. 'Yes, I'm ready. I'll just get my bag.'

Everyone said hurried goodbyes and the two of them then set off. Mal's dad's car was just a short walk along the road and soon the two of them were on their way to Lisa's house. The traffic was light and about ten minutes later they were parking in Acacia Road a few doors down from their destination. There was no sign of Sam's car in the road.

Before getting out of the car Mal's dad decided to talk over a suitable plan. 'I do think it best, Lisa,' he said, 'if we go to the door together. I am not anticipating finding anything untoward, but in view of the circumstances we find ourselves in, I think it for the best.'

'I think you're right,' was Lisa's reply. 'I do not know what to think, but what I do know is that I want to do the right thing and I am grateful to you for being here with me.'

'OK then,' said Mal's dad. 'Let's be off.'

With that they both got out of the car and walked up to the front door. Lisa rang the doorbell and then, putting her key to the lock, opened the front door, calling out as she did so. 'Hello, Sam. Are you at home?'

They entered the house quickly, but there was only silence. Between the two of them they checked every room.

In the kitchen there were a few unwashed dishes in the sink, but the bedroom was tidy. There was no evidence of a rushed departure. Mal's dad suggested that Lisa look to see if any of Sam's clothes were missing. A quick check revealed that in fact his favourite holdall was not in its usual place and it looked as though a small number of his clothes were missing. Lisa deduced that Sam must have left the house in his usual trainers. As far as Lisa could see Sam's credit cards and phone were not in the house.

'Right,' said Mal's dad. 'I think then we had better go to the station. Although Sam's phone does not have a tracking app, the police are able to track provided they have the phone number and the name of the service provider. That is our next course of action, I think.'

Lisa nodded. The two of them then locked the house and set off back to the car to drive to the station.

Once at the station, Mal's dad found somewhere for Lisa to wait whilst he went to speak with one of his colleagues armed with the details of Sam's mobile. It was not long before he returned and he then escorted Lisa into an interview room. The tracing had been carried out and Mal's dad explained that the location was about ten miles away in a village just west of Chelmsford.

'Can you think of any reason why Sam would be in that area?' Lisa was asked.

She thought for a moment. 'Do you know, I think I can. Sam has an old school friend, Alex, who lives on his own in that area, and it is just possible that he has gone to visit him. In fact, I think it is highly likely.'

'Right,' said Mal's dad. 'I think we will pay Alex a visit.

We won't phone in advance. We will just turn up and see if Sam is there. We will, I think, have to take another officer with us, though, because of the complexity of this case.'

'OK,' said Lisa. 'Let's hope we can get to the bottom of all this.'

Mal's dad then went to speak to a colleague again and after five minutes came back with another officer, also in plain clothes. DCI Miles was introduced to Lisa and they shook hands. With that the three of them made their way to the car and set off, each wondering what they would find when they arrived.

ELEVEN

With Lisa and Mal's dad on their way, David's mum wondered what the rest of them should do for the time up until lunch. As the dogs were ready for a walk, she ventured a solution.

'I know, why don't you all go over the brook and you can play football for a while on the grass? I will come as well with the dogs and I can take them for a walk. It will do us all good to get some exercise whilst we wait for news.' Everyone agreed and very shortly they were making their way over the bridge over the brook.

David's mum, Luna and Baz set off along the perimeter of the woods for a walk whilst the boys kicked the ball around. Just as David's mum was walking back to the boys, Daniel managed to kick the ball right into the woods. The other boys laughed and complimented him on the strength of his kick.

'I know,' said Daniel as he went to retrieve the ball. 'Why don't we take a walk in the woods? I'm getting too tired to kick any longer.' Everyone agreed, including David's mum, who was happy that the boys were enjoying themselves. They set off with David and Mal leading the way.

Soon it was apparent that David was actually leading the way. He turned to Mal and said, 'I don't know why, Mal, but I think we have to go back to where we found the bag.'

Mal smiled. 'Do you know, David, if you think that then I am sure you are right. You seem to have been right about so many things just lately.' With that he gave his friend a playful punch on the shoulder as they led the group into the woods.

Before long they came to the clearing where they had seen the two boys hide the bag. Somehow or other, David knew exactly where he wanted to look for whatever he had on his mind. He did not seem to be in any doubt. He felt around carefully in the undergrowth. Mal tried to help whilst the others stood around watching and waiting, wondering what was going on.

After a few minutes David stood up with something clasped in his hand. He held it out in front of him. 'I think I have found something,' he said.

'What is it?' said Mal. 'What have you got?' Everyone gathered round.

David explained, 'I don't know why, but once we started to walk into the woods it suddenly occurred to me that something had fallen out of the bag. Maybe something that the police did not expect to find in it and something we did not see when we looked. The feeling became stronger the further we walked into the woods.'

Mal was fizzing with excitement by this time. He asked again, almost shouting, 'Yes, David, but what is it?'

'Oh, sorry,' said David, who hadn't actually had the time to take a good look at his find himself. He then directed his whole attention to what he held in his hand. 'It seems to be some sort of ID,' he said. 'Looks like a membership card for something. Look, the name is quite clear. It says Frank Joiner.'

Mal then actually did shout. 'Don't put your fingerprints all over it, David.'

David stood stock still, not knowing quite what to do.

His mum, who had been silent until then, spoke. 'He's right, David. Here, slip the card into this clean tissue I have in my pocket. It will be safe then until we can get it to the police.'

David handed the card over to his mum, who very carefully wrapped it and put it equally carefully into her pocket. 'You know, David, you will probably have to have your fingerprints taken to eliminate you from the police enquiry.'

No-one knew at this point whether to look serious or to laugh. David started to laugh and so then so did everyone else.

'Come on,' said his mum. 'If you are sure there is nothing else here, we need to get on back to the house.'

The group started the trudge back to the house. They were all getting a little tired by this time except, Luna and Baz, who were enjoying themselves and still seemed full of energy. The boys were thinking about the exciting new find and, of course, their lunch. Halfway across the grass David's mum remembered that she needed to call Susan and Aylea to see how things were today and so she continued the walk home with her phone to her ear. All seemed to be well, with David's mum finishing off by saying she would pop by after lunch.

By the time they arrived back, there was still half an hour before lunchtime. The boys went into the garden to chill out, but the first thing David's mum did was to call Mal's dad. The call reached him just as he was parking the car west of Chelmsford, close to their destination, Alex's house.

David's mum explained what had happened that morning, how the boys had been playing football and David had then had a feeling that he really should return to where the bag had been hidden. She explained how he had searched through the undergrowth and found something. Mal's dad listened intently.

When the explanation had finished, he replied, 'Thanks. This is all really helpful. Please take care of the card – well, I know you will, but in the meantime, can you very carefully take a photo of it and send it to me? You need to handle the card only at the edges in case we need to take fingerprints.'

'Yes, of course. I can do that,' was the reply. I'll do it straight after our call.' She then asked how things were going at his end. Mal's dad reassured her and asked if she could let Daniel and Jake know that all was well.

'Of course,' was the reply.

Once the call was over and the photo sent, David's mum set about making lunch for everyone. Happily, there were a couple of pizzas in the freezer and they were soon on their way to the oven.

TWELVE

Mal's dad and the DCI were intrigued by the card that had been found in the woods. Lisa was asked if she had heard of anyone called Frank Joiner. Unsurprisingly she had not. Of course, the men mused, the location and finding of the card could be just a coincidence and totally unrelated to the present case. The DCI was unsure, but Mal's dad's gut feeling told him that it was not. The station was then called and asked if the name could be thoroughly checked and run through the police database. It was agreed to speed this through, and they were advised that they would be contacted as soon as information was to hand. With that dealt with the next task was to continue with the visit to Alex's house.

The small group parked a short distance from the house to give them a chance to survey the area and arrive quietly. Lisa had visited Alex with Sam many times over the years but only once or twice in the last couple of years. As they drew closer to the house Lisa spotted Sam's car parked in the driveway out of the way behind Alex's.

Lisa's footsteps were heavy as she walked up the path to the front door. Mal's dad rang the doorbell. Quite quickly the door was opened by Alex, who looked very surprised to see Lisa and the two men.

'Hello, Alex,' said Lisa. 'We came to see if Sam is here with you. I can see his car.'

'Yes, he is here,' said Alex, 'but who are your two companions?'

DCI Miles introduced himself and Mal's dad, and they both showed their warrant cards.

Alex nodded. 'You had better come in then,' he said, leading the way through the hall into the lounge.

Sam was sitting on the sofa but stood up quickly when everyone walked into the room. His eyes went straight to Lisa's. 'What's going on, Lisa?' he asked. 'Why have you come here and who are these two men?'

Lisa went to speak but was interrupted by the DCI, who did the introductions again and explained that they needed to talk to him about a serious matter.

Sam looked very flustered and worried. A bead of sweat formed on his brow. He stepped forward to Lisa and took her hands. 'I haven't done anything bad, Lisa. I promise. But everything has been so difficult lately. I came here to see Alex as you were away staying with your sister. I hope you and the boys are OK.'

'We are all fine, Sam,' said Lisa. 'Don't worry, but you really do need to speak to these two gentlemen. We can talk afterwards.' She then looked over at the DCI.

'Alex,' said the DCI, 'we are sorry to intrude, but is there somewhere we can have a quiet talk with Sam?'

'You can use this room,' replied Alex. 'I have some work to do in the study in any case. Would you like me to get you some tea, though?'

'Thank you,' replied the DCI. 'I think that would be good.'

With Alex off to the kitchen, everyone sat down. The DCI had indicated to Lisa that she should stay, as he felt her presence was relevant.

'Sam,' the DCI began, 'we need you to help us with our enquiries. This is a serious matter. I cannot emphasise too strongly how serious a matter this is. It is very important that you tell us the truth and that you hold nothing back.'

Sam looked very worried and looked backwards and forwards between the DCI and Lisa. 'I promise to tell the truth,' he said in a shaky voice.

'Firstly, can you please confirm that the red Peugeot outside this building including the letters GAG in its registration plate is yours?' asked the DCI.

'Yes,' confirmed Sam.

'Thank you,' said the DCI. He continued. 'We are currently investigating the theft of a bag containing some top-security material from a high-security establishment here in the UK. We have witnesses that confirm that this bag was, the day before yesterday, in your car which was parked in Acacia Road, where we understand you live. Fortunately, we now have the bag and its contents in our possession, but it is imperative that we find who stole it, how and why.'

The DCI paused. Sam's mouth had gradually dropped as he had listened to the DCI. A look of complete surprise and utter confusion crept across his face. 'What?' he blurted out. 'I had no idea. Oh, what on earth is going on? I just don't understand.'

'OK,' said DCI Miles. 'Sam, calm down. Just start, if you would, from the very beginning and explain to us exactly how you became involved in this and precisely what part you have played.'

Sam looked across at Lisa, took a deep breath and then started to speak, slowly and carefully, as if weighing up each word as if his life depended on it.

'Well. It all started with Covid-19. I was unfortunate to catch the virus but fortunate to recover fairly well. As you know, Lisa, I lost my job and it took me time to find another. It is not so well paid as the one I lost. I found myself in the position that many others found themselves in post-coronavirus. It became difficult to pay all the household bills and around Eastertime I needed some extra cash. A friend – well, I thought he was a friend – offered to make me a loan. I agreed readily and we planned that I would repay the sum gradually over the coming months. This, however, sounded easy but in practice proved to be quite difficult.'

'How much are we talking about, Sam?' asked the DCI at this point.

'£500,' Sam replied.

Lisa took a sharp intake of breath but did not speak.

Sam continued his story. 'All seemed well until a few weeks back when my so-called friend started to pressurise me, and I really didn't know what to do. He then put it to me that if I helped him out with a little job, he would forget all about the loan. It seemed like a solution to me. I guessed it was probably a little shady but decided to hear what he had to say before I made my decision.'

Sam then paused as there was a knock on the lounge door and Alex brought in a tray of tea. The DCI thanked him. The tea was passed around and then Sam continued.

'I guess it was a bit like one of those novels I read from time to time. Once you start to get involved it becomes very difficult to step back and say you don't want anything to do with whatever is going on. You know things, you have been told things and you find yourselves being drawn into something you want no part of. The plan was that my friend had to look after something, which he said was quite valuable, for a couple of days for a friend of his. He then had to pass it on to someone else. He wouldn't tell me what this item or package was, only that it was important. I tried to say I couldn't do it, but he became difficult and said he would tell Lisa about the money, so in the end I said OK. I really could see no other way out.'

'So, tell us what happened, Sam,' said the DCI.

Sam continued. 'I was asked to simply drive to Waterloo Station to pick him up with the item. This I did. He then asked me to drive back to Acacia Road. He said he was staying in a friend's flat for a few days whilst his friend was away on holiday. The flat was very close to where we live. When we arrived in Acacia Road his phone rang, and he got very agitated. He almost shouted at me that we had to get out of the car quickly and get up to the flat because someone was going to contact us. He almost dragged me across the road because he seemed to want to be inside the flat when the call came. In the hurry I left a car window open, although I did remember to lock the car. Once inside the flat his phone rang, and he took the call. He was very panicky. He said he had been asked to destroy the item and keep a low profile. He didn't seem to know what was going on. He asked me to go back to the car to fetch the bag, but when I got there, I saw that it had gone. I went back upstairs, and his panic reached a new level. We talked for a while and eventually he calmed down a bit. He then seemed to think that if the bag had gone, been stolen, then no-one could associate it with him or indeed me. He simply said that he was going to leave the flat and take himself off for a few days and he advised me to do the same. As you were away, Lisa, I rang Alex and came here. I have no idea who took the bag and frankly I didn't care or want to know.'

'What is the name of this man?' asked the DCI when Sam paused at the end of his long speech.

'His name is Brian Jakes,' said Sam. 'We just got talking in the pub near where I work when I went there one lunchtime. We seemed to have quite a few things in common. We met up a few times and to begin with I thought he was an alright guy.'

Just then the DCI's phone rang. He looked at the caller ID and, nodding to the others, said, 'I need to take this. I'll go out into the hall. I will be back in a minute.' With that he hurried out of the room with his phone to his ear.

The call to the DCI was from the station. All relevant checks had been run on the name Frank Joiner. The officer reported that there was no criminal record, but searches indicated that this man was employed by a high-security establishment in a senior position and had been in post for seven years. 'We need to interview this man with all possible speed,' said the DCI. 'Leave it with me for the time being. I will be back in the station very shortly.'

When the DCI returned to the lounge, he asked Sam, 'Have you any idea where Brian Jakes went?'

'No,' replied Sam. 'I didn't want to know where he went. I never want to see him again, actually.'

'Do you have a mobile number for him?' asked the DCI.

'Yes,' said Sam. 'I can give you that. I haven't tried to phone him and so I don't know if it is still working.' Sam then hastily took his phone from his pocket and gave the DCI Brian Jakes's phone number.

At this point the DCI felt it appropriate to reassure Sam. 'This is an unpleasant business, Sam, but I am able to inform you that we know who took the bag from the car and the culprits were simply two young lads who have been appropriately dealt with. Nothing or nobody sinister appears to be involved in that part of the theft.'

Sam looked slightly relieved.

'Right,' said the DCI. 'If you don't have anything to add, Sam, I will just need you to accompany us to the station to make a formal statement.' Sam looked slightly flustered at this but nodded in agreement. 'We can all go in my car,' said the DCI, 'and then I can arrange for a car to bring you back here if that is what you would like.'

With the interview over, Sam had a quick word with Alex and agreed to return later in the day. Lisa, Sam, the DCI and Mal's dad then took their leave and made their way back to the car to drive to the station.

On the car journey Lisa and Sam sat in the back together. They spoke to each other very quietly, almost whispering. Settling some of their differences, they agreed that after Sam had given his statement, he would collect his car from Alex's and go back home. Lisa agreed that she and the boys would also go back home that evening.

As they drew near the station it was agreed that they would drop Lisa off at David's house and that Mal's dad would pick up the ID card that the boys had found in the woods earlier in the day. This was quickly done, leaving Lisa back with her boys and Sam not long after arriving at the station to make his statement. Once at the station Sam was taken through to an interview room and Mal's dad sat down with him and another officer to take his statement. Meanwhile, the DCI went through to his office to proceed with the help of colleagues to endeavour to track down both Frank Joiner and Brian Jakes.

THIRTEEN

Back at David's house, David's mum offered Lisa some lunch, which she gladly accepted. Whilst she was making it, Lisa reassured Daniel and Jake that all was well and that they would be going back home that evening.

'Oh, that will be great,' said Daniel, 'but do you know what, Mum, I have quite enjoyed our little adventure and it is great staying here at David's house.'

Lisa smiled and replied, 'Well, it has certainly been interesting, and the hospitality here has been just great.'

Once lunch was completely out of the way and the boys were watching a film, David's mum told Lisa that she was just going to call next door to see how Aylea and Susan were getting on. Lisa agreed it was a good idea and said she would stay with the boys. David, hearing what was going on, said he would like to go and visit Aylea and Susan as well. David's mum found a spare packet of sugar-free biscuits in the cupboard, together with a carton of grapes she thought might make a nice gift, and then the two of them set off for the visit.

David's mum rang the bell and Aylea came to the door.

'Hello,' she said cheerfully. 'Please come in. Mum will be pleased to see you both.'

Susan was looking much better than the day before and Aylea too looked much more relaxed. Everyone began talking about everything that had been happening recently when Susan's mobile rang. She hurried over to the table and answered it, peering at the ID and giving the impression that she did not recognise the caller.

'Hello,' she said. There was then silence in the room as Susan listened to the caller with a puzzled expression on her face. 'Yes,' she said. 'Yes, it would be nice to see you, especially as we haven't seen each other for quite a while. Well, it is not really very convenient now, but...' She paused. 'OK, that will be fine. Yes, see you in about an hour then. Bye, Brian.'

Susan still looked slightly puzzled. She said, 'That was my second cousin, Brian Jakes. I haven't seen him for quite a while. We never got on that well, but for some reason he says he is in the area and would really like to call in to say "hello". I didn't think I could say no, really. He will be here in about an hour.'

'Oh, OK,' said David's mum. 'I suppose it is a nice thought to look you up, really. We won't stop too long then.'

At this point David remembered a book he had promised to give Aylea to read, so he said he would just go next door and collect it. Aylea asked if she could go with him and so off they went.

Next door the boys were still watching the film and Aylea sat down with them while she waited for David to find the book. Lisa was in the kitchen making some drinks and David went in there because, strangely enough, he thought he had left the book there.

'How are things next door?' asked Lisa.

'All good,' said David, 'although it was a bit weird. Susan had a call from a second cousin or someone like that who said he wanted to call round to see her this afternoon.'

'Oh, that's nice,' said Lisa. 'Who is that then? Do you know him?'

'No,' replied David. 'I have never heard of him. His name is Brian something. I know, Brian Jakes.'

Lisa suddenly dropped the plate she was holding. It fell to the floor but fortunately did not break.

David immediately saw there was a problem and cried, 'What's the matter, Lisa? Are you OK?'

Lisa did not exactly start shaking but very nearly did so. 'David, when is this man, Brian, supposed to be arriving?'

'In about an hour, Lisa,' replied David. 'Well, it will be less than an hour now, I suppose. What is the matter?'

'David, please go next door and stay with the others,' said Lisa. 'I need to make an urgent call. Please don't say anything, but make sure everyone, including Aylea, stays in the lounge.'

David nodded. 'OK, you can count on me. I'm afraid I sense it is all to do with what has been happening lately.' With that he went back into the lounge.

Lisa quickly called the station and asked for DCI Miles or Mal's dad. DCI Miles was on the phone in an instant. Lisa quickly explained what was happening, her words tumbling over each other.

'Right,' said the DCI. 'We will be there as soon as possible. Keep all the children with you.'

'OK,' said Lisa. 'Thanks. Please come as soon as you can.'

When Lisa returned to the lounge all the youngsters were intent on watching the film, except for David, who was looking out of the front window as if waiting for something to happen or someone to arrive.

Lisa went and sat with him. 'It's OK, David,' she said very quietly so that the others could not hear. 'The police need to speak to the man who is coming. They should be here very soon. Everything will be absolutely fine.'

Ten minutes or so passed. The film was only halfway through and so eyes were still glued to the screen. David and Lisa sat by the window. All seemed well. They were expecting the police to arrive any minute. They were beginning to get a little anxious, however, when they saw a tall dark man walking up the road towards Susan's house. He had longish hair and a worried look on his face. He stopped, looked to the left and to the right as if to check whether he was being followed. He then walked up the path to Susan's house. David and Lisa seemed mesmerised and almost glued to their positions by the window. The man rang the bell. Susan's door opened and the man went inside. Lisa felt panicky and thought she had to do something but couldn't think what.

The man had only been in the house for a few minutes or so when the door opened and he came out.

'What on earth has happened?' said Lisa. She and David looked at each other in bewilderment. 'We can't let him get away,' said Lisa.

Just then David thought of a plan. Before Lisa could stop him, he had rushed out of the front door and ran towards the man.

'Can you help me, please, sir?' he cried. 'I am at home on my own with my little brother and he has fallen and banged his head. Can you help, please?' The man looked flustered as if he really did want to help but knew he had to get away.

Just when David had run out of things to say and the man looked bent on ignoring his plea, there was a screech of brakes and a police car skidded to a halt. The DCI and Mal's dad jumped out. They ran towards Susan's house and the man they saw standing outside. The man saw what was happening and tried to brush David aside and make a run for it, but David stuck his leg out, receiving a hefty kick for his pains, but the man tripped and staggered sideways. He righted himself quickly and started to run down the road. Mal's dad gave chase and proved to be the faster of the two, quickly stopping and restraining him. He then marched him back to Susan's house.

'Good afternoon, sir,' said DCI Miles. 'Can I ask you please to confirm your name? We believe you to be Brian Jakes. Is this correct?'

'No, no, that is not me.' stammered the man. 'I'm—'

Just as he was about to speak Susan opened her front door to find out what all the noise was about. 'Brian,' she said, 'what on earth is all this? What is going on?'

Brian – for it was, of course, Brian Jakes – turned towards her and said, 'I am so sorry, Susan, I really did not want to involve you in all this. I am sorry, really.' He did indeed look sorry and Susan looked back at him with a look not of anger but of almost sympathy.

DCI Miles then spoke. 'Mr Jakes, we believe you can help us with some enquiries we are making of a serious nature. I am afraid I have to ask you to accompany me to the station.'

Brian seemed to shrink in size as his shoulders slumped and his head hung forward. 'OK, Officer. I'll go with you.' Brian nodded and half smiled at Susan, who seemed rooted to the spot. Jakes was duly formally cautioned and handcuffed, and Mal's dad accompanied him to the police car.

At this point the DCI had a brief word with Susan. He asked her why Jakes had visited her.

She explained, 'He is a second cousin and I have not seen him for simply ages. He phoned completely out of the blue an hour ago and asked if he could come to visit. I explained that it wasn't really convenient as I only came out of hospital yesterday, but he was insistent. When he arrived, he simply came in the house and said very little before he asked for money. When I said I did not have any to give him, he just said, "OK," and left. That is when you arrived.'

The DCI thanked Susan and with that he got into the car and they drove off to the police station.

By this time Lisa, Susan, David and David's mum were all standing outside the house.

Lisa was shaking. 'David,' she said, 'I told you. I told you all not to leave the room. Why did you rush out like that? Anything could have happened.'

'Sorry,' said David. 'I just knew I had to do something and there wasn't any time to think. Just time to act.'

David's mum stepped in. 'Lisa is right, David. You should not have run out when you did, but it was such a brave thing to do. I am so proud of you.'

David smiled. 'Well, the police got their man, didn't they? It was just like TV. Oh, but my leg does hurt where he kicked me!'

Everyone then fussed around David and his bruised leg.

Susan was looking very confused. 'I really do not know what all this is about. Can someone please explain?'

'Oh, sorry,' said Lisa. 'Everything has got in such a muddle. Can I come inside for a moment and try to give you some idea of what's been happening.?'

'Yes, please do,' was Susan's reply.

David's mum then said, 'Come on, David, let's get you home and have a look at that leg.'

David nodded.

'Lisa, if you have a brief word about what is going on with Susan, why don't you both then come back to the house and we can have some coffee?'

'Thanks,' said Susan, 'but after this I think I will need to sit quietly for a while. Please send Aylea back home when you are ready.'

With that David and his mum went into the house to see how the others were getting on, and Lisa and Susan stepped into Susan's house, where Lisa gave a brief rundown on events. After fifteen minutes or so Lisa returned to David's house, where the coffee was brewing.

The film was virtually over and when it ended the boys and Aylea all started to talk at once. David's mum had asked him to keep quiet about the events outside so as not to alarm anyone. There were drinks and biscuits all round until Lisa announced that it was probably time for her, the boys and Baz to return home. She thanked David's mum profusely for letting them stay overnight and everyone agreed to meet up again very soon. Lisa was feeling a little more relaxed and gradually got everything ready so that she could set off home. Her car was parked outside, David's dad having helped her fetch it the day before. Once everything was loaded in the car, goodbyes were said and Lisa set off home with her boys and Baz.

After a while Luna made everyone aware that she wanted a walk and so David and Mal decided to take her, and Aylea asked if she could tag along too. This the boys readily agreed to. They wandered over the bridge to the grass and spent time messing about for almost an hour. When it was time to return home Aylea said goodbye at her house and went in to join her mum. David and Mal returned to David's house to find that David's dad was home from work and that dinner was being prepared. Mal stayed for a while, then said, 'Cheerio' to everyone and set off home with the usual promise to be back again first thing in the morning. Both boys were wondering quite what the next day would bring.

FOURTEEN

By the time the officers and Brian Jakes arrived at the station, Sam had left, having made his statement and been advised that he should not leave the area until further notice. Sam had been honest and cooperative in making his statement. He was feeling rather stupid and apologetic about getting involved in the whole sorry business in the first place. A car had taken him back to Alex's, where he had explained briefly what had happened. Alex's reaction was a mixture of shock and sympathy, but after a frank talk over coffee they remained firm friends. Before long Sam had got his things together to drive home, where he was looking forward to seeing Lisa and the boys and starting afresh.

When Jakes arrived at the station, he was shown straight into an interview room. He was offered coffee and was required to wait in the presence of a uniformed officer. DCI Miles went straight to check with colleagues to see what progress had been made in tracking down Frank Joiner. He was advised that Joiner had been located and was in police custody in Salisbury. This was pleasing news.

DCI Miles then made his way to the interview room where Jakes was waiting. He was accompanied by another colleague, DI Jones. Jakes was asked if he wished to have a solicitor present. Jakes shook his head and said, 'No, thanks,' very slowly, then thought for a moment, changed his mind and said, 'Yes, yes, please.' He was asked if he wanted to call his own solicitor or whether he would like the duty solicitor to be present. Jakes decided that the duty solicitor would be suitable and there was a short delay in commencing the interview whilst he was located and briefed.

DCI Miles commenced the interview by explaining to Jakes what was known so far. Jakes listened carefully. He admitted that he had asked Sam to collect him by car from Waterloo Station together with a package. He claimed that he did not know what was in the package but that he had been asked to keep it safe for a friend. When asked if he thought the package had been stolen, he hesitated, thought for a moment and then said, 'Well, I suppose I knew that it was, but I was not told what it was and I really didn't want to know. I just wanted to carry out what was asked of me and be recompensed as arranged for my time.'

DCI Miles then asked who had given him the package and Jakes fell silent. The duty solicitor then advised him to answer the question. Jakes still remained silent.

The DCI then asked, 'Do you know someone called Frank Joiner, Mr Jakes?'

Jakes jerked his head back in surprise and it was obvious from his body language that he did. After a moment or two he answered, 'Yes,' and slumped forward in his seat with a hangdog expression.

'Was it Joiner who gave you the package to look after?' asked DCI Miles.

'Yes,' replied Jakes, looking totally dejected. He gave the impression of a man who knew the game was up.

The DCI continued. 'How do you know Mr Joiner?' he asked.

'I have known him a long time,' Jakes replied. 'When I used to live in Salisbury, his wife was a friend of my ex-wife and so we went out for meals and so on. I always found him interesting to talk to. He has a scientific background. Much different to my own profession in IT.'

'So, have you kept in touch much since you moved to London?' the DCI asked.

'Yes,' replied Jakes. 'We keep in touch from time to time and meet up occasionally.'

'So, how did it come about that he asked you to look after a parcel for him?' was the next question.

'Well,' said Jakes. 'He called me and asked if I would go down to Salisbury, meet him for lunch and then bring something back to London for him and keep it safe until he was able to collect it. I thought it a little strange. He then said it was important and that he could not explain any more but that he would let me have a couple of free weeks in his villa in Spain for a holiday when the job was done and he came to collect the parcel. He said it was an arrangement he had with someone and it was something to do with his work. I sort of thought it odd but could not really see any harm in it. I thought the gift of a free holiday was quite generous for a simple task, but times have been hard lately and as I couldn't really afford a holiday this year, I thought I would do as he asked.'

'Can you explain, please, why you needed to enlist someone's help?' the DI asked.

'I needed to travel by train because I do not have a driving licence at present and my friend impressed upon me the need to keep the item safe, which meant avoiding tube trains, buses, taxis and travelling on foot. Sam Arnold seemed the obvious person to ask and he jumped at the proposition when I put it to him.'

Just then there was a knock on the door and an officer entered the interview room with a note for the DCI, which he quickly read. He then stood up, nodded to his colleague and said, 'Interview suspended at 4.30pm. Please stop the tape.'

The officer explained that there was an urgent call for him from Salisbury and that the caller was holding on for him on the phone in his office.

When the DCI reached the phone and sat down to speak, his Salisbury colleague advised him that the call was high security and asked him if there was anyone who could overhear him. The DCI replied, 'Negative.'

The Salisbury officer then went on to explain that Frank Joiner had been interviewed in the presence of the duty solicitor. He had admitted taking from the establishment where he worked, without permission, items of top-security status and passing them to Brian Jakes with a view to collecting them from him at a later date. He stated that he had not told Jakes what was in the package and had asked him not to open it. He had further added that for reasons he had not yet given, he had asked Jakes to destroy the package instead of keeping it in safe custody for him. Further, he had no idea how his name had come to the attention of the police if it had not been given to them by Brian Jakes. The interview had been suspended when Joiner had become uncooperative in answering some key questions. He was, of course, still in custody and the interview would be resumed later that day.

The DCI pondered over what the officer was saying and concluded that Jakes had certainly not opened the package as it was still sealed inside the bag and therefore could not have known what was in it unless Joiner had told him. The DCI explained that he was currently interviewing Jakes, who, it seemed, was probably just a pawn in a much bigger game.

The conversation concluded, the DCI returned to the interview room.

The DCI resumed the interview with Jakes by asking, 'Can you explain, please, what happened when you arrived back in Acacia Road with Sam Arnold and the parcel?'

Jakes replied, 'Just as the car stopped and we were about to get out my mobile rang. It was Frank. He sounded in a dreadful panic. He wanted to talk but then it sounded as if someone had come up to him to talk and so he hurriedly said he would call me back in a few minutes. His call made me panic and so I said to Sam that we had to get up to the flat quickly so that I could take the call. We had not been inside for more than a minute or two before my mobile rang again. It was Frank. He sounded just as agitated as before. He just asked me to destroy the bag and its contents, not explaining how I should do that. He then said that I was to lie low for a few days and hung up before I could say hardly anything at all. I sort of yelled to Sam to get the package, but when he returned to the car it was gone. I didn't know what to think, but it then dawned on me that something bad was going on, so I decided to get out of the area as soon as I could and advised Sam to do the same. In my panic I lost my wallet and could think of nothing else other than to get some funds somewhere local, and that was when I phoned Susan.'

The DCI then asked about the card with Frank Joiner's name on it. 'I must confess,' said Jakes, 'Frank gave me a card of his whilst we were having lunch. I should have put it in my pocket, but I got a little confused. I was sorting my things out for the journey back to London. I was supposed to turn the bag Frank had given me inside out, only I forgot, and I must have put the card inside the bag. I remember now the bag had a distinctive logo. It's where Frank works.'

The questioning of Jakes continued and in Salisbury it was not too long before the interview with Joiner was resumed. The evening wore on with the officers getting closer to the truth around a crime that, if successful, could have had serious consequences for the realm.

FIFTEEN

After dinner David reflected that this was the strangest summer holiday of his short life so far. It had all been rather exciting. He never quite knew what to expect next and he knew that Mal felt the same. He had a quiet evening with his mum and dad reflecting that that was just what he needed. Too much excitement getting David too much out of his routine was not good for him and his blood sugar.

David didn't go to bed late. He was actually rather tired and so he did not need telling twice that it was time for some shuteye. He happily went upstairs, went to the bathroom and then climbed into bed, falling asleep almost before his head touched the pillow.

The first part of the night for David consisted of dreamless sleep. Something, however, woke him. It was still very dark. He listened for a while and even climbed out of bed and looked out of his bedroom window but saw nothing amiss. After a minute or two he presumed all was well and so he went back to bed and fell asleep again almost immediately. This time, however, he started to dream.

He was walking along in the dark and then gradually it slowly started to get lighter and so he increased his pace. After a minute or two it was fully light, and David found himself in what appeared to be an office. There was a large picture window overlooking an area of grass and many trees. A man was standing in front of him by what was presumably his desk. The man looked bewildered and, yes, a little frightened. Gradually David felt himself drawn into the man's thoughts. What he found there was unnerving. *What have I done?* thought the man. *What on earth have I got myself into? I never should have listened. I am afraid and, yes, I am ashamed. I must stop it now.* He then reached for his phone, checking no-one else was around and made a call. He had barely said two words when someone entered the office without knocking. The man hurriedly ended the call with the words, 'This is important. I will call you again in five minutes.'

David's vision started to fade, and he gradually felt himself drawn back into the darkness. He felt as if he was floating gently on the sea, lying on his back and looking up at the stars. He didn't seem to be going anywhere until, strangely, he was aware that he was in the hall at home. There was a knock on the door. His mum opened it and there were three men standing there. They were smiling and asked if he and Mal were there in the house.

'Yes,' said his mum. 'Please do come in.'

The next thing David was aware of was someone shaking his hand and giving him something. There was a huge smile on Mal's face and then everything dissolved into shimmering silver stars.

David slipped deeper into slumber and did not wake until the next morning when his dad called out to him to wake up.

David made his way down to breakfast. He could remember his two dreams fairly clearly, but he thought it was probably best not to mention them. Well, certainly not to his mum and dad, anyway. Mal, of course, was a different matter. He was not sure what they would find to do today but thought it might be worth putting it to Mal that they take a bike ride. His leg was still a bit sore and bruised from the day before, but it was not really bothering him. They could take Luna, unless his mum wanted to take her for a walk. As he was eating breakfast his mum reminded him that they had an appointment at the doctors at four o'clock.

'OK,' David replied. 'I had forgotten, but I will make sure I am home in time.'

When Mal arrived strangely enough he had thought to bring his bike and so the plans for the morning were clear. David's mum felt like a walk and so she said she would take Luna with her. The boys made some sandwiches for themselves and filled their water bottles. They both wanted to talk about recent events but agreed they would cycle to one of their favourite spots and then sit down to talk. Before long they were on their way. David's leg was aching a bit, but he didn't let on to Mal.

Once they had arrived at their destination they sat down and relaxed. Both were thirsty and so each took a swig from their water bottles. There was such a lot to talk over. Mal had not really heard anything new from his dad. All the boys really knew was that men were being questioned and that the bag they had taken to the police contained something very important. That, they reflected, made them feel very important. They felt certain that eventually they would learn more, but they also surmised that none of the grownups would ever tell them the full story. That was often the way with grownups, they reflected. Eventually they ate their sandwiches and then it was time to cycle back to David's so that he was not late for his appointment.

When they arrived back at David's house his mum was getting ready to drive to the doctors. David didn't really like these visits but knew he had to do them. He always felt a little embarrassed that he wasn't able to do his own injections, but the doctor was always very kind and very pleasant. Today, though, he was particularly nice as he explained again about how to do the injections and David left feeling a lot more confident and he sort of agreed that he would try again. His mum was very encouraging. He began to feel that it wouldn't be too long before he could manage it.

Back home it was a quiet evening, with David and his dad taking Luna for a walk whilst his mum went next door to see how Susan and Aylea were getting on.

SIXTEEN

There were still almost three weeks of the summer holidays left, but with most of the excitement and adventure over, the days for David and Mal settled into a pleasant but fairly uneventful routine. The boys met up and played some football with Harish, Ali and John, and they also spent some time with Daniel and Jake. They went over to the woods and spent time in their usual haunts, sometimes taking Aylea with them. None of the youngsters could really decide whether or not they were looking forward to going back to school and starting secondary.

As predicted, a clear explanation of what had actually happened with the mysterious bag and the men involved never quite came the way of David and Mal, although it was impressed upon them more than once by Mal's dad that the whole issue had been dreadfully serious and a sort of disaster had been averted. Mal thought that something should have been in the newspapers about it, but his dad had ticked him off and told him not to be so silly.

So the holiday continued to take its course until one

day just three days before school was due to start there was a knock on David's door, and when his mum answered there were three men: Mal's dad, DCI Miles and another man who introduced himself as Chief Constable Jarrold. David and Mal, who were just chilling out in front of the television, stood to attention almost like soldiers when the three were escorted into the room by David's mum and the introductions made. Mal looked with questioning eyes at his dad.

'Shall we all sit down?' said David's mum. 'Would you gentlemen like some tea?' she asked.

'Thank you. That would be excellent,' replied the chief constable. 'But first of all, may I explain to these two young men why we have called around to see them today?'

'Of course.' David's mum nodded.

'Well, boys,' began the chief constable, 'I have come here today with my colleagues to thank you both personally for the parts you played in putting right an incident that without your help could have caused serious harm to the realm. I am unable to go into details because of high-security restrictions, but rest assured your help has been both recognised and valued. For this reason, we have come here to present you each with a chief constable's special award, which I hope you will both be happy to accept.'

Mal's jaw dropped so low he was simply just gaping at the chief constable, whilst David sat quietly remembering his dream of several nights past.

David was the first to speak. 'Oh, that's just amazing,' he said. 'That's my dream come true.'

'It must be,' uttered Mal, still in shock.

'Thanks ever so,' both boys then said almost simultaneously.

The chief constable then reached into his briefcase and took out the two awards. He stood up and, without being asked, David and Mal stood up too. The chief constable then shook hands with each of the boys and presented them with their awards. The three of them then sat down to the sound of clapping from the others in the room.

'That was simply wonderful,' said David's mum. 'I'll now go and fetch the tea.'

'Now I know why you wanted us to wait in this morning, Mum,' said David, and then they all laughed.

DCI Miles and the chief constable did not stay too long, but it was long enough for them to enjoy the refreshments made for them and to talk to the boys a little about police work.

Before the visitors left David surprised them by saying, 'I am pleased the man – Mr Joiner, wasn't it? – changed his mind. I suppose then he wasn't such a bad man after all.'

David's mum looked questioningly at him, as did the others.

'Oh, I just had a dream. That was all!' said David.

The chief constable looked as if he was about to speak but then seemed to think better of it. Goodbyes were then said, and David and Mal were once again alone in the lounge with David's mum.

'Well done,' said David's mum. 'You can take your bikes off for that ride now if you want.' Both boys smiled and after a while off they went.

The next few days passed quickly and soon the boys

were back into a school routine, although having moved to secondary, the routine was different than before. Both found their feet quickly and when, after a few days back, there was an announcement in assembly about their special awards, the boys felt doubly confident about life in their new school and their future.

As for David, he found that he now had the confidence to do his own injections. Yes, he was different from other boys his age and he still had strange dreams, but as far as he was concerned, they only made life more interesting.

D157884